AROUND CHI-TOWN

Anyone wondering where last night's unexpected June heat wave came from need look no farther than the posh downtown hotel where a couple dozen of the hottest men in Chicago were auctioned off for charity. (For charity—or for the hundred or so hungry females in the audience?)

And the star of the show was our own Justin Connelly. Though this member of the famous Connelly clan hides inside the hallowed halls of his family's corporation, he is definitely *not* all work and no play! Looking positively studly in his black tux, Justin attracted the highest price tag of the night.

Society debs from the renowned Novak, Powers and Barlow families upped the ante, but it was an unknown bidder who snared the baffled bachelor. Reliable sources identify Kim Lindgren as Justin's very own secretary. Can't you see it now? "Miss Lindgren, take a memo.... Check on the status of the research data, follow up with the advertising figures, and...while we're at it, come give your boss a kiss."

After all the Connellys have been through of late—with son Daniel's assumption of the throne of Altaria, his attempted murder, the corporation's near computer disaster—yours truly guesses even this blue-blooded family could use a bit of fun and folly!

Dear Reader,

Summer vacation is simply a state of mind...so create your dream getaway by reading six new love stories from Silhouette Desire!

Begin your romantic holiday with *A Cowboy's Pursuit* by Anne McAllister. This MAN OF THE MONTH title is the author's 50th book and part of her CODE OF THE WEST miniseries. Then learn how a Connelly bachelor mixes business with pleasure in *And the Winner Gets...Married!* by Metsy Hingle, the sixth installment of our exciting DYNASTIES: THE CONNELLYS continuity series.

An unlikely couple swaps insults and passion in Maureen Child's *The Marine & the Debutante*—the latest of her popular BACHELOR BATTALION books. And a night of passion ignites old flames in *The Bachelor Takes a Wife* by Jackie Merritt, the final offering in TEXAS CATTLEMAN'S CLUB: THE LAST BACHELOR continuity series.

In *Single Father Seeks...* by Amy J. Fetzer, a businessman and his baby captivate a CIA agent working under cover as their nanny. And in Linda Conrad's *The Cowboy's Baby Surprise,* an amnesiac FBI agent finds an undreamed-of happily-ever-after when he's reunited with his former partner and lover.

Read these passionate, powerful and provocative new Silhouette Desire romances and enjoy a sensuous summer vacation!

Joan Marlow Golan

Joan Marlow Golan
Senior Editor, Silhouette Desire

Please address questions and book requests to:
Silhouette Reader Service
U.S.: 3010 Walden Ave., P.O. Box 1325, Buffalo, NY 14269
Canadian: P.O. Box 609, Fort Erie, Ont. L2A 5X3

And the Winner Gets...Married!

METSY HINGLE

Silhouette® Desire®

Published by Silhouette Books

America's Publisher of Contemporary Romance

Special thanks and acknowledgment are given
to Metsy Hingle for her contribution to
the DYNASTIES: THE CONNELLYS series.

For Missy & Molly Brown,
My Four-Legged Babies Who Provide Continuous Joy

 SILHOUETTE BOOKS

ISBN 0-373-76442-1

AND THE WINNER GETS...MARRIED!

Visit Silhouette at www.eHarlequin.com

Printed in U.S.A.

Books by Metsy Hingle

METSY HINGLE

is an award-winning, bestselling author of romance who resides across the lake from her native New Orleans. Married for more than twenty years to her own hero, she is the busy mother of four children. She recently traded in her business suits and a fast-paced life in the hotel and public-relations arena to pursue writing full-time. Metsy has a strong belief in the power of love and romance. She also believes in happy endings, which she continues to demonstrate with each new story she writes. *The Wager* (MIRA Books, August 2001) was Metsy's first single-title release. *Behind the Mask* (December 2002) will be her second MIRA Books title. She loves hearing from readers. For a free doorknob hanger or bookmark, write to Metsy at P.O. Box 3224, Covington, LA 70433.

MEET THE CONNELLYS

Meet the Connellys of Chicago—
wealthy, powerful and rocked by scandal,
betrayal...and passion!

Who's Who in
AND THE WINNER GETS...MARRIED!

Justin Connelly—His head is always buried inside a
column of figures at Connelly Corporation. But this
budding bachelor is about to become intrigued by
"figures" of a different kind...the *female* kind!

Kimberly Lindgren—In business suits and upswept
do's, she's toiled side by side with her boss, Justin.
Until one night when she lets her hair down and allows
him to see she has more to offer than good typing skills!

Robert Marsh—A loyal Connelly employee and fiancé to
a Connelly woman. What lies beneath his million-dollar
smile and prep-school education?

One

"**W**here is he?"

Kimberly Lindgren jerked her gaze up from the computer screen as Tara Connelly Paige stormed into the office suite. "Mrs. Paige," she said, quickly coming to her feet to intercept the other woman, who, given the high color in her cheeks and the snap in her voice, was obviously furious. "I don't think your brother is expecting you."

"Oh, I'm sure he's not. But he *is* going to see me."

After working as an executive assistant for more than two years at Connelly Corporation, Kim had become a master at smoothing ruffled Connelly feathers. Yet something about the fire in this particular Connelly's violet eyes told her this was not going to be one of those times. Still, she had to at least try. "I believe Justin is on the phone at the moment," she said, positioning herself in front of her boss's office door. "If you'll have a seat, I'll let him know that you're here."

"Thanks. But I'll just tell him myself."

Kim didn't move. "That might not be a good idea, Mrs. Paige. Your brother's had a rather difficult morning." Which was an understatement if there ever was one, Kim admitted silently. The day had turned into a disaster—one for which she felt partly responsible since it had been she who had discovered the cost overruns in the firm's new advertising campaign that was set to kick off next month.

"If that's your way of telling me that Justin's in a rotten mood," Tara went on, "I appreciate the warning. Really, I do. But it just so happens that I'm in a rather foul mood myself, and Justin is the reason. I *am* going to see him, Kim. Now the only question is whether you're going to move away from that door and let me pass or am I going to have to go through you?"

Stunned, Kim remained speechless. For several long seconds she simply stared at the petite dark-haired woman dressed in the chic red suit, dashing hat and gloves and killer high heels. At five foot seven, Kim estimated she had at least five inches and twenty pounds on Tara Paige. Yet Kim didn't doubt for a moment that the other woman meant every word she'd said.

"It's your call, Kim. What's it going to be?"

"Why don't we go in together?" she suggested, seeing no alternative. Since Justin really was on the telephone, she tapped on his door and entered without waiting for a response. The sight of Justin at his desk with the magnificent view of the Chicago skyline behind him was something that never failed to make her heart race. But the scowl on his handsome face now made her tense. Glancing past him, Kim noted the storm clouds threatening outside the windows. While she didn't like to think of herself as superstitious, she got a sudden sinking sensation in her stomach.

Of course, having an obviously upset Tara on her heels didn't help.

"Listen, Marsh, I don't care how busy you are with the wedding plans. I want the revised budget and copies of all your correspondence with Schaeffer on my desk by the end of the day. Is that clear?"

Kim nearly winced at the edge in Justin's voice, but it was the way he was rubbing the back of his neck that concerned her. He'd been working too hard again, she thought. Since taking over as vice president of marketing six months ago when his brother Daniel had assumed the throne of Altaria, he'd handled the work of two men. He'd also had to deal with more than his share of problems—beginning with the attempted assassination of his brother, followed by the corporation's computer crash a few weeks ago, and now this latest fiasco with the firm's advertising campaign. The fact that the error started with Robert Marsh, who was about to become Justin's brother-in-law, surely added to Justin's stress.

"I mean it, Marsh. I want everything before the close of business today or you can clear out your desk," he said, and slammed down the phone. Only then did he look up at her. "Kim, I—" He looked past her, and upon spying his sister, his scowl deepened. "I said I didn't want to be disturbed."

"I know, and I'm sorry for the interruption," Kim began, knowing all too well that Tara couldn't have come at a worse time. "But your sister needed to speak with you, and I thought maybe you could see her for a moment before you leave for your next appointment."

"Mother was right about you, Kim. You really are a diplomat," Tara said as she breezed past Kim and placed herself directly in front of Justin's desk. Despite Tara's refined demeanor and tone, Kim sensed the anger still simmering just beneath the surface. "The truth is that, short of tackling me, Kim did everything possible to keep me out of here."

"And naturally you refused to take no for an answer," Justin replied.

"Naturally. And considering it's a skill I learned from you, big brother, I can assure you that I have no intention of taking no for an answer now."

Kim held her breath as Justin and his sister squared off. While she'd always found the size of the Connelly family mind-boggling, it was the dynamics between the siblings that continued to fascinate her. Probably because her own family had consisted of just her and her mother—and now, only her. Suddenly feeling like an intruder, Kim said, "I'll leave you two alone."

"You might as well stay," Justin replied before she'd taken a step toward the door. "This shouldn't take long and there are several things you and I need to go over before I leave." He glanced at his watch. "All right, Tara. I've got all of five minutes to spare. So why don't you tell me what's got you so fired up?"

"I'm fired up, brother dear, because you think you've weaseled your way out of being in the bachelor auction fund-raiser this weekend like you promised."

Justin sighed. "It's not a question of my weaseling out of anything. I simply can't do it."

"Why not? And don't hand me that lame excuse that you gave Jennifer about some unexpected business problem that you need to take care of, because I'm not buying it."

Kim held her breath as temper flashed in Justin's hazel eyes.

"It's not an excuse. It's the truth," Justin countered. "Whether you believe it or not is up to you."

"Well, I don't believe it," Tara returned.

"Suit yourself," Justin told her, and picked up a report from his desk. "Now, if you'll excuse me, I've got work to do."

"I will not excuse you, Justin Connelly," Tara said. She slapped the gloves clutched in her fist against her opposite palm like a whip. "And don't you dare pull that 'I'm too busy' number on me. Have you forgotten how important this fund-raiser is? That the money is going to be used to help the families of slain police officers?"

Tara didn't have to add "families like Jennifer's," Kim thought, because they all knew that until Jennifer's recent marriage to Chance Connelly, the former social secretary and her young daughter had been one of those families. That Justin remembered, too, was evident from his somber expression.

"No, I haven't forgotten," Justin said firmly. "I've already apologized to Jennifer for pulling out at the last minute. But I have an important meeting in New York that afternoon, and it would be nearly impossible to get back in time."

"Then change the meeting or go a day earlier or next week."

"Don't you think I would if I could?" He raked a hand through his hair. "I had a difficult enough time getting this meeting on Friday and it's something that can't wait. If you're worried about the money my pulling out will cost, I've already assured Jennifer that I'll be sending a generous contribution to make up for canceling."

"And just how do you propose we make up for the money that we'll lose in ticket sales when word gets out that Justin Connelly, voted one of Chicago's most eligible bachelors and the key draw for the blasted event, has pulled out of the auction? Of course, that doesn't even begin to take into account the amount of money that we might have been able to raise if your tush were on the auction block.''

Justin frowned at his sister. ''You make me sound like a side of beef.''

Tara sat down on the corner of Justin's desk. ''In a manner of speaking, you are.''

''Thanks a lot.''

Tara shrugged. ''Can I help it if there are women out there willing to pay big bucks for the chance to spend an evening with you? Face it, pal, you're a hot commodity. Not only are you the brother of a king, but you're also an heir to the Connelly fortune. You wouldn't believe the number of women who actually think you've got a pretty face and sexy body. And judging by the comments I've heard, they'd all like nothing better than the chance to get you between the sheets.''

''For Pete's sake, Tara! Will you knock it off?'' Justin snapped, his face heating. Pushing away from his desk, he rose and walked over to the windows to stare out at the rain that had begun to fall.

''Well, if this isn't a first. I do believe I've embarrassed you.''

He whirled around, shot her a withering glance. ''Of course you've embarrassed me. And Kim, too,'' he added. ''Since when do you and your friends sit around discussing men as though they were...were...''

''Sex objects?'' Tara offered.

Justin glared at her.

Tara laughed. ''Oh, come on, Justin. Did you really think that was a privilege reserved only for men?''

''You're my little sister!''

''I'm twenty-five years old, a widow and a mother,'' Tara said, her voice suddenly serious. ''Believe it or not, I do know a thing or two about sex.''

Justin groaned. "I don't want to hear this," he told her, and, returning to his desk, he snatched up the report in front of him. "I've got work to do. I'm truly sorry about the fund-raiser, but I promise I'll send a sizable check."

"What about the auction?"

He sighed again, put down the file. "Tara, I've already explained, there's just no way I can make it," Justin said, and there was no mistaking the regret in his voice at having to deny his sister's request. "I'll admit, I've never been wild about the idea of being in this auction. I only agreed to do it because Jennifer and Mother asked me to and I know it's for a good cause. But as much as I hate letting them or you down, there is simply no way I can be in two places at once."

Kim hadn't been any keener on the idea of Justin spending a romantic evening with some beautiful socialite than he seemed to be, she admitted. And she had been relieved when he'd canceled. But now, witnessing Tara's disappointment and Justin's distress at being the cause of it, she couldn't help but feel guilty. Before she could change her mind, Kim blurted out, "Actually, there is a way you can do both."

Both sets of Connelly eyes turned to her. "How?" Tara asked.

Kim swallowed. "A couple of things would have to be worked out first, but it is possible."

"What do you need?" Tara countered.

"First you and Jennifer would have to arrange it so that Justin would be the last bachelor to be bid on at the auction."

"That's not a problem," Tara assured her. "What else?"

"Justin's meeting scheduled here Friday morning with the marketing department would have to be postponed until next week."

"That shouldn't be a problem, should it?" Tara asked her brother.

"I guess not." He eyed Kim warily. "What about Schaeffer?"

"Your New York meeting with him could be moved up a few hours. Say a meeting over lunch instead of one that spilled over into the dinner hour."

"What makes you think Schaeffer will agree to that?" Justin asked. "I had a devil of a time getting that meeting in the first place."

"I've gotten to be sort of friendly on the phone with Mr. Schaeffer's secretary," Kim said. "She works closely with him. I think I can get her to convince him that it would be...beneficial to have an early meeting and leave his evening free."

"I see," Justin said.

Kim felt her own face heat at the knowing look in his hazel eyes. "That way even if your meeting with Mr. Schaeffer runs over, as long as you made it to the airport by five o'clock or five-thirty, I can get you on a shuttle that would put you back in Chicago in three hours. Allowing thirty minutes travel time to get you from O'Hare to the hotel, you could be there for nine o'clock."

"And I can have a driver waiting at the airport to pick you up and take you to the hotel," Tara concluded. She clasped her hands together and smiled. "Please, Justin, say you'll do it."

"Seeing how my assistant has conspired with you, I don't seem to have much choice."

Tara turned to her and beamed. "Bless you, Kimberly Lindgren. I owe you one."

"Not at all. I was glad to help."

"You did a great deal more than help," Tara insisted before turning back to Justin. "The woman's not only a diplomat, she's a genius, Justin. I wonder if you realize how lucky you are."

"I'm beginning to."

Something in Justin's voice and the way he was looking at her caused Kim's pulse to race. Mortified that he might realize how she felt about him, she averted her gaze. "I'd better go see about making those calls," Kim told them.

"And I've got to go or I'll never make it to that meeting on time," Justin replied and began shoving papers into his briefcase.

"But we have to discuss your date package," Tara informed him even as he snapped the briefcase shut and reached for his suit jacket. She followed him to the door. "We need to come up with something really special."

"Get with Kim," he told her. "She'll know what to do."

"I think dinner and tickets to the theater would be nice," Kim suggested a few minutes later.

"Nice, but not special," Tara informed her. "If a woman is going to bid top dollar for a date with Justin, we need to offer her something exciting."

Just being on a date with Justin would be exciting enough for her, Kim mused silently. But then she was in love with him and had been for months now. Not that Justin had any clue about her feelings for him. He didn't. And for that she was eternally grateful. After all, what could be more cliché than to have a secretary fall in love with her boss—a boss who didn't even know she existed?

"Any ideas?"

Kim gave herself a mental shake and reminded herself to deal in reality. "How about one of those dinner cruises?"

"Hmm. That would be romantic. But I was hoping for something different," Tara replied. She crossed her legs and began to tap one manicured nail against her chin. Suddenly her finger stilled, and, tilting her head to the side, she stared at Kim. ''If *you* were the one going on a date with Justin, where would *you* want to go?''

Kim stiffened. Had Tara somehow picked up on her feelings for Justin, she wondered. ''Me?''

''Yes, you.''

''Really, Mrs. Paige, I don't think—''

''Please,'' Tara said, wincing. ''Do you think you could manage to call me Tara? I'm guessing that we're about the same age, but every time you call me Mrs. Paige I feel like someone's grandmother.''

Kim's lips twitched. ''You don't look like anyone's grandmother.''

''I certainly hope not,'' Tara told her with a laugh.

The woman was beautiful, glamorous, sophisticated. Everything that she wasn't, Kim thought. And even though at twenty-four she was only a year younger than the other woman, Tara had already been married, widowed and had a child. Kim couldn't help but think that life was passing her by quickly.

''So what would you consider a fun and exciting date?'' Tara asked.

''I doubt that my idea of fun and excitement would appeal to the women who'll be bidding at the auction.''

''Why not?''

''Because I'm not like them,'' Kim answered honestly.

''You're a woman, aren't you?''

''I...yes.''

''Then whatever appeals to you should appeal to other women.''

''But—''

''No buts,'' Tara told her and stood. She gathered up her

purse and gloves. "I've got to run. But why don't you put a date package together that would appeal to *you*."

"Like what?"

Tara shrugged. "I don't know. Something that *you* would like to do if you were the woman going out on a date with Justin. Make it as simple or elaborate as you want."

"But what if I choose something that's all wrong?"

"You won't," Tara assured her. "Trust your instincts, Kim. Whatever you choose, I'm sure it's going to be perfect."

"Let's hope you're right," Kim told her and wished she had as much confidence in herself as Tara seemed to have in her.

"I am," Tara said with a smile and started toward the door. She paused, turned back. "Oh, I almost forgot. Are you doing anything Friday night?"

"No," Kim replied cautiously.

"Great. I've purchased a couple of tables for the fund-raiser, so I have some extra tickets. Would you do me a favor and attend as my guest?"

"But Mrs.— Tara," she corrected when the other woman gave her a reproving look. "That's very kind of you, but I couldn't possibly go."

"Why not? You said you were free."

"I am, but—"

"No buts. You deserve to enjoy yourself after all your hard work, and you'd be doing me a favor by going. Will you need a ticket for an escort?"

"Uh, no. That won't be necessary." It had been months since she'd been out on a date—and couldn't even fathom whom she would ask to accompany her to something like this.

Tara beamed at her. "Great. Then I'll see that a ticket is messengered over to you in the morning."

Before Kim could argue further and tell Tara that she really didn't belong at such an affair, the other woman was gone.

"Damn it!" Justin pitched the report he'd been reading onto the others on his desk. How he would dearly love to wring Robert Marsh's neck. Unfortunately, he couldn't because the man had covered his tracks well. Frustrated, Justin shoved away from his desk and wandered over to the windows that filled one wall of his office. Normally looking out at the skyline soothed him, helped him to organize his thoughts. Yet watching the shifting colors as the sun began its descent seemed to make him even more restless. Probably something to do with the gloomy weather that had played havoc with the city most of the day, he told himself.

Of course, this mess with Schaeffer hadn't helped. It was going to take a miracle to launch the marketing campaign on time without blowing an even larger chunk of the budget. But somehow he had to find a way, Justin reminded himself. He simply had to. His family was counting on him. Sighing, he returned to his desk and dug in, determined to find that miracle.

More than two hours later, when he lifted his head, Justin gave a grunt of satisfaction. By shifting and scaling back expenses, he'd managed to make some progress and he'd done so without losing the integrity of the plan. Now, if he could bring the rest of the costs into line, he just might be able to pull it off. Rummaging through the papers on his desk, he searched for the file folder containing the billing costs on the marketing campaign to date. Unable to find it, he stopped and tried to recall when he'd had it last. He'd given it to Kim to check out the accuracy of some of the figures, he remembered. Maybe it was still on her desk.

Intent on finding the folder, Justin started out of his office only to stop cold at the sight of Kim. For once she wasn't sitting at her desk, the picture of efficiency in her sensible heels and sedate business suit, hard at work. Instead she stood in her stocking feet with her blouse opened at the neck and her eyes closed while she stretched. And as he watched her extend and stretch her body, all thoughts of the missing folder and business went right out of Justin's head.

In the six months that he'd worked with Kim, she had been the perfect assistant. Not only had she made the difficult task of taking over after his brother's departure for Altaria a smooth one, but her people skills had proven invaluable to him. In all that time she had been poised, efficient, businesslike.

She didn't look the least bit businesslike now. Not with her eyes closed, her head tipped back and a serene expression on her face. Slowly, as though performing a dance, she began to bend her body. And if his life depended on it, Justin couldn't have looked away. Transfixed, he watched her move with the grace of a prima ballerina. When she folded her body in two, her skirt climbed up, and Justin swallowed hard at the view of her legs. Funny, he thought, as Kim brought her head down to press against first one ankle and then the other, but he'd never noticed before just how long and shapely Kim's legs were. And how in the devil had he failed to notice what a small waist she had? Or the enticing lines of her hips?

Justin's blood heated as she unfolded her torso and reached over her head once more, pulling the silky white blouse she wore taut against her breasts. He must have been blind, he decided, not to have realized how lushly curved

Kim was. He noticed now—a fact that was all too evident by the desire stirring in his gut.

Don't be a jerk, Connelly. Say something. Let the woman know she isn't alone.

Justin opened his mouth, intent on announcing his presence, when Kim removed the clip from her hair. He nearly swallowed his tongue as yards and yards of long, honey-blond hair came tumbling down around her shoulders and face.

Sweet heaven, had all that gorgeous, sexy hair been tucked into that no-nonsense twist?

Damn! He scrubbed a hand down his face. He'd always been a sucker for a woman with long hair, beginning with Miss Malone, his kindergarten teacher. Biting back a groan, Justin admitted that next to Kim, Miss Malone wouldn't even stand a chance.

He was absolutely out of his mind, Justin assured himself. He squeezed his eyes shut and tried to block out this new image of Kim. Didn't he have enough on his plate to deal with without this? They'd yet to find out who had tried to assassinate his brother, and he was none too thrilled about his sister Alexandra's upcoming marriage to Marsh. Add to that the problems at work and the headaches resulting from that most-eligible-bachelor status. The last thing he needed was to complicate his life even more with a woman—especially a woman he worked with on a daily basis.

The smart thing to do was to go back to his office and forget he'd ever seen this side of Kim. Which was just what he intended to do, Justin decided as he opened his eyes. Allowing himself one final glimpse of the sensual creature before him, he started to retreat into his office when Kim opened her eyes and stared straight at him.

"Justin," she said his name in a breathless whisper that

did nothing to cool the erotic thoughts that had been running rampant through his head only moments before.

"I'm sorry," he managed to get out. "I didn't mean to disturb you."

"You didn't. Disturb me, I mean," she added while she slipped back into her shoes. "I was…I was just doing a few stretching exercises to try to work out some of the kinks in my shoulders and neck."

Although she told him something about the importance of stretching, the words barely registered because he was far too mesmerized by her attempts to tame all that honey-gold hair into a neat twist. As far as he was concerned, she'd failed big-time, since several thick strands managed to escape the clip and now tumbled carelessly down her nape and the sides of her face. With her cheeks flushed and her hair mussed, Justin could all too easily imagine the way Kim would look after a night spent making love.

Kim took a breath. "Anyway, I guess I got kind of stiff sitting at the computer and— And here I am babbling on. Did you want me for something?"

Justin nearly groaned at the innocent remark as totally inappropriate thoughts came to mind. "No, I was just…" Damn, he couldn't even remember what it was he'd come out here to look for in the first place.

"Justin, are you all right?"

No, he most definitely wasn't all right. Not when he couldn't shake the punch of arousal he'd experienced upon seeing Kim stretching a few moments ago.

"Is something wrong?"

Justin gave himself a mental slap, forced himself to focus on the present. "No. Nothing's wrong." He let out a breath. "It's been a long day. And speaking of long days, what are you still doing here?"

"I had some work that I wanted to finish up."

"Whatever it is, it can wait until tomorrow. You should have left hours ago," he said, more gruffly than he'd intended.

"You're still here."

"My family owns the place," he pointed out.

"Yes, of course. I never meant to imply...I'll leave now and get out of your way," she murmured, then quickly turned away.

But not before Justin caught a glimpse of hurt in those big blue-green eyes. Damned if he didn't feel as though he'd just kicked a puppy. "Kim," he said, moving beside her. He turned her around to face him and tipped up her chin. "I'm sorry. I didn't mean that the way it sounded. Just because I'm in a lousy mood is no reason to take it out on you."

"It's okay."

"No, it's not." He captured the fist she held stiffly at her side and lifted it between them. "If it'll make you feel better, go ahead and sock me one," he said, jutting out his chin. "I deserve it for acting like a jerk."

"You're not a jerk."

"Sure, I am. Or at least I gave a good impression of one a minute ago. I hurt your feelings, and for that I'm sorry."

"But you didn't—"

Justin silenced her with a look. "You may be a terrific assistant, Ms. Lindgren, but you're a lousy liar."

"Thank you. I think."

He grinned at her. "Hey, I'm the one who should be thanking you. The truth is I'm not sure what I'd do without you."

"Oh, I'm sure you'd manage just fine," she said, and reclaimed her fingers. Though she stepped back, she came up against the desk, which prevented her from putting the distance between them that Justin suspected she'd intended.

"Hopefully, I won't have to find out. But seriously, what I should have said, and botched totally, is that as much as I appreciate all your hard work, there's no reason for you to put in such long hours."

"I don't mind," she told him. "I like my job. I like working with you."

"Darned if I understand why," he countered, and smiled at her again. "But how about calling it a day? I bet if you try, you might still be able to book yourself a massage at the health club."

"I probably could if I belonged to a health club. But since I don't, there's really no reason for me to hurry," she said, smiling up at him.

The smile intrigued him almost as much as she did. There was something both innocent and seductive about her smile. And it did nothing to ease his arousal. Taking a step back, Justin tried to shake off this new awareness of Kim as a desirable female.

"You're scowling at me again," she accused.

"Not at you. At myself," he corrected, feeling like an idiot. Of course she didn't belong to a health club. The fact that his family and most of his friends worked out regularly at a club certainly didn't mean that Kim did the same. Chances were she couldn't afford that kind of luxury. Because a luxury is what it was. It was the reason he refused to join the fancy clubs and worked out at a hole-in-the-wall gym. He stared at her and suddenly realized that other than the fact that Kim was single and had no family—facts his brother had told him when he'd taken over the position of vice president of marketing—he knew very little about Kim's personal life despite the fact that they worked so closely together. It was hard to imagine her all alone when he had such a large family himself. "I guess this is my night for apologies. That sounded terribly arrogant of me.

I shouldn't have assumed that you belonged to a health club.''

"Don't be silly. It was a logical assumption.''

"No, it wasn't. And I'm sorry if I embarrassed you.''

"You didn't,'' she insisted. "Please. There's nothing to be sorry about. Connelly Corporation is very generous to its employees, and most of the clerical staff belongs to health clubs or spas. I could, too, if I wanted.''

"But you don't want to?''

She shrugged. "I just don't know when I'd get the chance to use it.''

"Which is my fault.''

She tipped her head, studied him. "And how do you figure that?''

"Look what time it is and you're still here. I work you too hard.''

"No, you don't. Besides, I don't work nearly as hard as you do,'' she countered.

Justin snorted. "I don't have a choice. My family is depending on me. You, on the other hand, don't have any excuse. I mean it, Kim. No more late nights like this for you.''

"But I told you, I like my job. I like working with you.''

"Even when I'm a royal pain in the neck?'' he teased.

"Even then,'' she said. "Now, unless you need me for something, I'd really like to finish transcribing these notes,'' she told him, and reclaimed her seat in front of her computer screen.

"The notes can wait until tomorrow.''

"They could, but there's no reason why they have to.''

"Correct me if I'm wrong, but which one of us is the boss here?''

Kim laughed. "You are. But all I need is ten minutes to

finish, and then I promise I'll head for home and a long, hot soak in the tub.''

An image of Kim naked in a bathtub covered only in bubbles had Justin gritting his teeth. ''Scouts' honor?''

''Scouts' honor,'' she said and held up three fingers.

''All right. You've got ten minutes and then I want you out of here.''

''You got it,'' she promised and went back to work.

When Justin exited his office fifteen minutes later, Kim was still at her desk, staring at her computer screen and rubbing the back of her neck with one hand.

Even though his brain told him it was a mistake, he started toward her. ''Here, let me do that,'' he said, and pushed her hand away and replaced it with his own.

''You don't have to do this,'' she argued.

Justin ignored the comment. ''No wonder you're hurting. Talk about tense. Relax,'' he commanded, and began to massage her shoulders. Determined to prove to himself that his earlier reaction to Kim had been a fluke, a momentary aberration caused by spending too much time at work and neglecting his social life, he went to work on those stiff muscles. Satisfied that, by analyzing the situation, he now had any earlier sexual attraction he'd experienced toward Kim firmly under his command, Justin skillfully tackled the mass of knots along her spine. Using his thumbs, he applied pressure to a particularly tight spot between her shoulder-blades and began to knead it.

''This really isn't necess— Oh...''

His control slipped a notch at the sounds coming from Kim. Steeling himself, Justin reminded himself this was Kim Lindgren. Kim his assistant. Kim his right hand. Kim, whom he had no right to think of as a woman. But when she moaned again, his body reacted. Desire fisted in his gut, sent heat firing through his veins.

So much for being a master of control, Justin decided. Calling himself ten kinds of fool, he tortured himself further by inching closer and breathing in her scent. Roses, he thought as he dragged in another whiff. Since when had the scent of roses become a turn-on?

But he forgot all about the way she smelled when Kim tipped her head forward, giving him further access to her neck. Although he knew he was playing with fire, he reached for the strands of hair trailing her nape. They slid across his fingers like wisps of silk and did nothing to cool his blood.

The sight of that pale strip of skin where the edge of her blouse ended sent another wave of heat rushing through him. Before he could stop himself, he moved his fingertips along her bare neck. Soft and warm was all he could think. And before he could shut off the voice in his head, he heard the question. *Would she be this soft and warm all over?*

"You have magical hands," Kim murmured.

The husky timbre of her voice stripped off another layer of his control. "Kim, I—"

The sound of the elevator bell in the hall outside the suite sent sanity rushing back. Saved by the bell, Justin thought, and dropped his hands to his sides. Taking a step back, he dragged in a steadying breath just as the building's chief of security entered the suite.

"Evening, Mr. Connelly. Ms. Lindgren," Tom Jenkins said.

"Good evening, Tom," Justin told the other man.

"Hi, Tom," Kim said softly.

"I'm just making my rounds. You folks going to be here awhile longer?"

"I'll be here for another hour or so, but Ms. Lindgren is

leaving now. As a matter of fact, I'd appreciate if you'd see her to her car.''

''Sure thing, Mr. Connelly.''

''But, Justin, my notes—''

''Can wait until tomorrow,'' he said briskly. ''You've put in enough hours for one day. Go home, Kim. I'll see you in the morning.''

Kim's expression fell, and he could have sworn it was disappointment he read in those blue-green eyes. But before he could change his mind, he turned on his heels and retreated to his office, where he sat down at his desk and dropped his head into his hands.

Talk about close calls. He was lucky, Justin assured himself. He'd come dangerously close to crossing the line with Kim just now, and tomorrow he would be grateful he hadn't done so. Because if he'd kissed her as he'd wanted to do, he had no doubt he would have made a major mistake on both a personal and a business front. Silently patting himself on the back, he told himself he'd done the right thing. He'd done the noble thing. He'd walked away when every instinct in him had wanted to pull her close, taste her mouth.

Yes, he was lucky, he reiterated. They both were. Lifting his head, Justin stared unseeingly at the work spread out across his desk. And as the memory of Kim's scent, the feel of her skin came back to haunt him, Justin grimaced and decided that sometimes doing the honorable thing really sucked.

Two

Justin was just being kind. Don't read anything into it.

Kim repeated the words like a litany—just as she had been doing since she'd left the office hours earlier. Not that it seemed to be doing her much good, she admitted. Because, try as she might, she hadn't been able to stop thinking about the way Justin had been looking at her just before Tom's arrival. Not as a boss would, but the way a man looks at a woman. A woman he wants. And she'd felt the heat of those oh-so-serious hazel eyes trained on her like a caress.

Even now, just remembering that look in his eyes made her shiver with excitement, with longing. Despite her limited experience with men, she knew desire when she saw it. And it had been desire she'd read in Justin's eyes. Desire for her.

Her. Plain, polite and boring Kimberly Lindgren.

A ripple of pleasure raced over Kim even as that nagging

voice inside her reared its head and warned her not to be foolish, not to delude herself by believing that Justin would ever see her as anything more than his assistant.

Be realistic, she told herself. The man was a Connelly. A member of one of Chicago's most prestigious families. Wasn't he just voted one of the city's most eligible bachelors? The man dated models, socialites, gorgeous women— not nobody secretaries with less than sterling pedigrees.

But, lying in the darkness of her bedroom with morning still hours away and her thoughts so filled with Justin, she ignored the warning voices. For once she didn't want to be the sensible and level-headed Kim Lindgren. Instead she wanted to relish the memories of how Justin had looked at her, touched her. Snuggling beneath the covers, she squeezed her eyes shut and allowed herself to relive those magical moments at the office with him. The feel of his hands—so strong, yet gentle. The warmth of his breath tickling her neck as he stood behind her. The hot, hungry look in his eyes when she'd turned around and met his gaze.

Kim clasped her hands to her throat as the image of his face swam before her closed lids. He'd been standing so close to her, close enough that she could see the faint trace of stubble darkening his chin. Close enough for her to smell the woodsy and spicy scent that he always wore. Close enough for her to feel the warmth of his body just inches from her own.

Her heart raced. That ache she got low in her belly whenever she dreamed of how it would be to have Justin hold her in his arms, to have him tell her that he loved her as she loved him, started anew. "And the chances of that ever happening are about as likely as Chicago getting snow in July," she muttered as sanity returned at last.

Grabbing her pillow, she flopped over onto her stomach and ordered herself to go to sleep. And in sleep she allowed herself to play out the fantasy as she never dared do when she was awake. In the safety of slumber she imagined the feel of his mouth—hot and hungry on hers—tasting her, filling her, and then the sound of his voice as he whispered words of love and called out over and over, "Kim...Kim..."

"Kim? Kim, did you hear me?"

The impatient note in Justin's voice startled Kim from her musings. Embarrassed to be caught daydreaming, she looked up and found a somber Justin standing in front of her desk. "Sorry. What was that?"

"I asked if you had a chance to draft that memo of understanding for my meeting with Schaeffer on Friday."

The all-business note in his voice lashed at her like a whip. "It's on your desk in your in basket," Kim answered, doing her best to match his cool tone.

"Good," he grumbled, and started toward his office only to pause and look back at her. "Are you feeling all right? You seemed...distracted."

Kim flushed. "I'm fine. I've just had my mind on putting together that date package for the bachelor auction so I can messenger it over to your sister today," she told him, opting for the half-truth. She had been working on the package, but it hadn't been the real source of her distraction. Justin had—or rather she'd been busy daydreaming that she was the lucky woman who would get to share the date with him.

He groaned. "Don't remind me. I still can't believe I let Tara convince me to go through with that thing instead of just sending a check."

"Your sister's very persuasive."

"Pushy is more like it."

Deciding not to comment on what seemed to be a family trait, she pointed out, "It *is* for a good cause."

"Which is the only reason I agreed to do it in the first place," he informed her, and mumbled something about needing to have his head examined because he'd probably be changing clothes in the limo to get to the thing on time.

Given Justin's reluctance to participate in the auction, Kim suddenly questioned her decision to follow Tara's advice and make the date one that she herself would find appealing. "Do you want to take a look at what I put together as your date package?" she asked, and picked up the envelope that contained a certificate that detailed a romantic sailing date on Lake Geneva.

"I'm sure it's fine," he told her, and started again toward his office.

"It'll only take a minute to look it over, and I'd—"

"I said it's fine," Justin snapped.

Kim clamped her lips together and remained silent.

Justin sighed, rammed a hand through his hair. "Listen, I'm sorry. I didn't mean to bite your head off. It's just that...I have a lot on my mind at the moment."

"I understand," Kim replied, still stinging from his sharp tone. She did understand that Justin worked much too hard, that he demanded too much of himself. In the six months that she'd worked with the man, she had seen him in a number of stressful situations. But never once during that time had he ever raised his voice to her or spoken to her as he had a moment ago. Even worse, she hadn't realized until now just how vulnerable she was to him or how much he could hurt her.

Was it because of last night? she asked herself. Had he somehow picked up on her feelings for him and was now uncomfortable with her?

Mortified at the thought that Justin might know she was in love with him, Kim wished she could simply disappear.

"Kim, I really am sorry," he told her again, his expression softening. "The last thing I would ever want to do is hurt you."

Kim nodded and averted her gaze, afraid she would see pity in his eyes, afraid of what he would see in hers.

He stood there a moment longer, then said, "I'll be in my office the rest of the afternoon. Please hold my calls."

"But what about the lunch with your father?"

"I canceled it so I could work on this Schaeffer deal. I'll need to schedule some time with him when I get back from New York."

"I'll take care of it," she advised him, pleased that her voice could sound so professional and detached when inside she still felt raw, exposed.

"Thanks," he said, and disappeared inside his office.

But the instant the door closed behind him, Kim lost some of the starch in her spine. So much for any notions that something had happened between them last night, she thought. Hoping that Justin might finally have begun to see her as more than just his assistant was obviously nothing more than a fantasy on her part. A fantasy that bore a painful resemblance to her mother's string of hopeless romances. She'd adored her mother, missed her still. But as much as she had loved her, she had hated the constant highs and lows caused by her mother's endless quest to find Mr. Right.

Evidently she had more of Amanda Lindgren's penchant for impossible dreams than she'd thought, Kim decided. Thank heavens she also possessed enough common sense and pride to choke a mule. Whatever change she'd thought she'd detected in Justin's attitude toward her last night, it obviously wasn't romantic in nature. There hadn't been anything remotely romantic about the way he'd looked at her today. If anything, he'd seemed cool and unapproachable—not at all the warm, caring man she'd grown accustomed to working with these past months.

Taking a cue from Justin, she promised herself that no matter how she felt about him, he would never know. She picked up the envelope containing the certificate for the bachelor auction. After enclosing it in a transmittal envelope, she started to attach a cover note to Tara declining the offer of the ticket. Then she hesitated. Maybe she would think about it some more. She tackled the pile of letters and messages on her desk, determined to bury herself in work and forget about those magical moments with Justin last night.

"What else?"

"I need you to sign off on these letters and the checks that go with them," Kim informed Justin two afternoons later.

Quickly he scanned the letters in question, noted the sums of the accompanying checks and scrawled his signature across the documents where indicated. As he did so, he steeled himself against her scent—a whiff of roses and something exotic—that filled his head each time he was near her. "Is that everything?"

"Except for the final draft on the Schaeffer document. I've put in the additional changes you wanted, but you'll probably want to go over it one more time to be sure everything's covered."

She handed him the lengthy document he'd worked and reworked several times already, and as she did so, his fingers brushed hers. Kim snatched her hand away—but not before he'd felt that stab of awareness again. "I'll take a look at it now, then maybe you can get out of here at a decent time, for a change."

"I'll be at my desk."

After she'd exited his office and he was alone again, Justin swore. Something had to give—and soon. Ever since the other night, Kim had been acting differently toward him. Oh, she still was doing a great job as his assistant. He couldn't have asked for anyone more knowledgeable, efficient or reliable. But he sensed a distance now, a wall, that hadn't been there before. While he...he had been going slowly insane with very nonbusinesslike thoughts about her. Despite the fact that he'd driven himself relentlessly at the office during the day, then pounded on the bags at the gym until he was exhausted in the evenings, he'd lain awake for the past two nights thinking about Kim, wanting her. Try as he might, he hadn't been able to forget the image of her the other night. Sighing, he sat back in his chair and closed his eyes.

And there she was again with her hair tumbling down her back and shoulders. He curled his hands into fists, remembered how silky that hair had felt, how soft and warm her skin had been. He dragged in a breath and could have sworn he could smell her—that sweetness of roses and sunshine and secrets.

Get a grip, Connelly.

Justin snapped open his eyes. He had to stop thinking of Kim that way, he reminded himself. Maybe the trip to New York would help. Surely spending all day Friday, plus the weekend away from Kim would help him get his head and hormones straight. And who knows, maybe that bachelor auction would turn out to be a blessing in disguise. With a little luck he just might meet someone interesting. Maybe another female would make him forget all these wild thoughts he'd been having about Kim, Justin decided. And with that plan of action firmly in mind, he picked up a pen and went to work on the agreement.

"That should do it," Justin muttered some time later. He tossed down his pen and leaned back in his chair. Finally, after incorporating several suggestions from his father and fine-tuning the document once more, he was satisfied. Now he just needed to sell it to Schaeffer. Stretching to ease the stiffness in his shoulders, he cupped his hands behind his head and spun his chair around to face the windows.

"Aw, hell," he grumbled at the sight of the star-filled skyline. A quick glance at his watch told him he'd been at it for hours, which meant that Kim had been forced to stay late again. Shoving out of his seat, he tore out of his office.

"What's wrong?" Kim asked, jerking her gaze up from the computer screen.

"It's late, and I promised that you'd get out of here at a decent hour for a change."

"It's only half past eight," she informed him, and averted her gaze.

"Only? You're supposed to be able to leave at five." He could probably count the times on one hand that she'd left at quitting time. He claimed a seat on the corner of her desk. "And thanks to me, you've had to work late again."

"I didn't mind. I had some things I needed to catch up on. So did you finish?"

"Yes," he told her, but made no attempt to give her the agreement.

Finally she shifted her gaze back to his for a moment. "If you intend for me to put in those changes, you're going to have to give that to me," she said, and held out her hand for the document.

"I'll plug in the changes. Just pull up the original agreement on the screen and then you can get out of here."

"Don't be silly. I'll do it," she argued.

"No. Go on home. You've stayed late enough."

Kim hesitated a moment. "Justin, is there something in that agreement that you'd prefer I not know about?"

"Of course not."

"Then since it is part of my job, I'll make the changes," she informed him. "Besides, as you'll recall, the last time you used my computer, you, um, had some difficulties."

"That wasn't my fault," he said, recalling that the system had ended up crashing when the terminal had insisted he'd performed an illegal operation.

"I'm sure it was just a coincidence. All the same I'll feel better if you let me make the changes."

Reluctantly Justin handed over the pages.

She scanned the edited sections a moment. "It'll probably take me about twenty minutes to do these and print up a fresh copy. If you want to go home, I can drop the revised set by your apartment on my way home."

He found the idea of Kim visiting his apartment appealing. Which was why he said, "I'll wait."

When his stomach grumbled a few seconds later, Kim looked up. "Maybe you should go down the street and have dinner while I take care of this. By the time you get back, it'll be finished."

"What about you? You haven't eaten yet, either. And don't tell me you're not starved because I wouldn't believe you."

"I'm all right," she said as she continued to scroll down on the screen and make changes. "I'll pick myself up something on the way home."

"Do you like pizza?"

"Yes," she said, pausing, her voice cautious, as were her eyes.

"Everything on it?"

"Justin, this isn't necessary."

He ignored her and reached for the phone. After dialing information, he had the number connected. "Everything on it?"

She frowned at him. "No anchovies."

Justin grinned at that. "You're a girl after my own heart, Kim Lindgren," he told her, and placed an order for a super-size pizza extravaganza with everything except anchovies.

"You shouldn't have done that," she admonished. "I'll never be able to eat even a third of that pizza."

"Good. That means there's more for me."

"But I thought…"

"You thought?" Justin prompted.

"I thought you would prefer to sit down to a real meal, something from a nice restaurant."

"By a 'real meal' I take it you mean a thick steak or some expensive entrée with a fancy sauce served on china?" Justin countered.

"Yes."

Justin grinned at that. "You obviously don't know many teenagers, do you?"

She gave him a puzzled look, which caused her brow to wrinkle in the most adorable way. "No."

"Well if you did, you'd know that pizza isn't only considered a real meal. It's the best meal possible."

Justin had been right. The pizza was a fabulous meal, especially when it was accompanied by an enormous Italian salad, bread sticks and a glass of wine from the bar in his office. Kim couldn't remember when she'd enjoyed a meal half as much.

Maybe it was the wine, she thought, as she breathed in the merlot and watched Justin over the rim of her glass. He seemed more relaxed, warmer toward her than he'd been in days. And she…she was enjoying herself, enjoying him. Sitting back in her chair at the conference table in Justin's office, Kim allowed herself the pleasure of watching him.

"How's the wine?" he asked.

"Wonderful," she replied, and took another sip to prove it. Remembering what she'd read about wine, she allowed the flavor to rest on her palate to fully enjoy its taste before swallowing.

"Don't tell me you're full," Justin teased.

"Hardly." She took a third slice of the pizza. "Tell me more about the teenagers you work with at the youth center."

"They're a challenge," he began, and told her about how bright some of the troubled teens he'd been working with really were. "They keep me on my toes, that's for sure. You should think about coming down. There's a lot they could learn from you."

"I doubt that. You're the marketing whiz."

"But there's more to business than marketing. You're smart, organized and you have a way of putting people at ease. Those are rare qualities, Kim. You instill even a fraction of them in those kids and it'll go a long way toward shaping their future."

"Thank you," she murmured, touched by the sincerity of his words.

"Nothing to thank me for. It's the truth. And I hope you'll at least think about coming down to the center."

"I will," she promised, and nearly choked when he smiled at her. God, but he was beautiful, she thought as she watched him tackle another slice of pizza. With that hint of red in his brown hair, the hazel eyes filled with laughter, the strong cheekbones and stubborn chin. For him to be so nice and honorable, too, just made him that much more attractive. Who could blame her for falling in love with him?

"You going to eat that?" he asked, pointing to the last slice of pizza on her plate.

"No. You go ahead and finish it," she told him.

"Tell you what. Why don't we split it," he suggested, and proceeded to divide the slice in two.

Justin polished off his half in a matter of seconds, but it took her a while longer. "Full?" he asked as he refilled both of their glasses.

"Stuffed is more like it," she confessed, dropping her napkin on the paper plate.

"Hang on a second. You've got a little tomato sauce on your face."

"Where?" she asked, and reached for a napkin to blot at her chin.

"Here, let me do that," he said, and, taking the napkin from her, he caught her chin in his hand and gently dabbed at a corner of her mouth.

He was so close Kim could see the stubble on his chin, smell the woodsy scent he wore. And when his fingers stilled and he looked into her eyes, she could scarcely breathe.

"You have the most incredible-colored eyes," he told her.

"They're blue."

"No. Not blue. Not green. But a combination. They're the color of water in the Caribbean where I sailed my boat last summer."

He stroked her cheek with his thumb, brought his face a fraction closer. "Kim, I..."

Kim's heart beat wildly in her chest. The breath stalled in her lungs. Instinctively she tipped up her head, closed her eyes and waited for the touch of his mouth.

"I-it's getting late. We probably should call it a night," Justin said, and dropped his hand from her face.

The words hit Kim like a blast of cold water. Her eyes snapped open and she scrambled to her feet, horrified of what Justin must think of her. Unable to meet his gaze for fear he would realize she'd wanted him to kiss her, she began to frantically snatch up the empty plates and napkins. "You can go on home. I'll clear away this stuff and lock up," she told him as she piled the paper goods atop the now-empty pizza box.

"Here, let me get that," Justin offered when her unsteady fingers began dropping the soiled napkins.

"I've got it," she argued.

But Justin ignored her. "You've worked hard enough today. Go ahead and close up shop at your desk while I handle the cleanup."

Eager to escape, Kim didn't argue. She simply fled Justin's office, praying she could get out of there before he saw the tears prickling at the backs of her eyes. Quickly she grabbed her purse from inside the drawer of her desk where she kept it and snatched up her car keys. "Good night, Justin," she called out, and started for the door. "Thanks again for dinner."

"What? Wait a minute," he said, sticking his head out the door of his office. "Let me get rid of this," he told her, indicating the wineglasses and wine bottle he held in his hands. "It'll only take me a second and then I'll walk you to your car."

"That's really not necessary. Tom or one of the other security guards will see that I get there safely."

"But—"

"I've got to go. Have a safe trip and good luck with Schaeffer tomorrow," she said, and exited the office suite quickly before the first tears began to fall.

Three

"Kim, wait!"

The door swooshed closed behind her. But not before Justin had a chance to see her face. Had those been tears in her eyes? he wondered. Were they because of him? Had Kim realized what he'd been thinking of doing a few moments ago? What he *still* wanted to do?

Damn!

Staring at the door through which Kim had just exited, Justin checked the urge to go after her. He scrubbed a hand down his face. To do so would be a mistake, he reasoned. He'd come dangerously close to kissing her a few minutes ago. Were he to follow her now, he wasn't at all sure that he wouldn't give in to the desire that had been nagging at him for days.

Definitely not a good idea, Connelly.

Not only would he risk losing the best assistant he'd ever worked with, but Kim would have every right to slap him and the company with a sexual harassment suit. Still, for a moment there, he'd almost believed that Kim had *wanted* him to kiss her.

Right! More like wishful thinking on his part, Justin conceded as he headed back into his office. Kim probably hadn't given him a second thought. She'd certainly never indicated that she had any romantic interest in him. Why should she? Despite that most-eligible-bachelor tag he'd been labeled with, the truth was he was a dull guy who spent most of his time working and little time on fun. If women were drawn to him, it probably had more to do with the fact that he'd been lucky enough to be born of a gene pool that provided him with decent looks. Being a part of the Connelly dynasty that had amassed a fortune and having ties to royalty didn't hurt, either. Kim, on the other hand, was a bright and attractive young woman. No doubt any number of guys were interested in her. And while he knew little about her personal life, it stood to reason that there would be a man in her life.

Justin frowned at the notion of Kim in the arms of another man. Disturbed by how much the idea bothered him, he told himself it was because he was protective of Kim. After all, they worked closely together. He'd become fond of her, valued her as his assistant and depended upon her. It was only normal that he should feel some concern about her, he reasoned.

He was going to drive himself crazy if he didn't stop thinking about Kim and whom she might or might not be involved with. Determined to wipe Kim and thoughts of her love life from his mind, Justin focused all his attention on making sure he had everything he would need while he was in New York.

For the next ten minutes the impending business meetings drove all other thoughts from his mind. After adding two other file folders he would need for his meetings in New York, as well as the redrafted contracts for the Schaeffer deal, he surveyed the contents of his briefcase.

"I'm forgetting something," he muttered. But what?

Don't forget your Palm Pilot.

Justin jerked his head up as he remembered Kim's earlier instructions. Striding out of his office, he marched over to Kim's desk. There was his Palm Pilot resting in the caddy where Kim had placed it when she'd taken the hand-held computer gadget in order to synchronize it with the updated data on his computer's main network. He picked up the palm-size marvel that contained not only his schedule for the entire year, but also the addresses and phone numbers of his family, friends and business associates. As he turned to leave, he spied the single white rose on Kim's desk that she'd bought from a street vendor the previous day.

And quick as a wink she was back in his head again.

Only this time she wasn't at Connelly headquarters. She was on the beach with her faced tipped up to the sun and her lips turned up in a smile. She'd exchanged the neat, ladylike blue suit she'd worn that day for a pair of shorts and a T-shirt that made the most of those curves he'd caught a glimpse of the other evening. And instead of that prim, sleek twist, her hair was loose and flowing like silk in the wind. But it was Kim's eyes—those serious blue-green eyes that had been haunting him for nearly a week—that he saw most clearly. Those eyes were bright with laughter and expectation and desire.

Justin's mouth went dry. He sucked in a breath. "Oh, man." He definitely needed to get a grip, he told himself, and strode back into his office. He tossed the Palm Pilot into the briefcase, then snapped it closed and forced himself to shut off the enticing images of Kim in his head.

He was going to be in serious trouble if he didn't get a

handle on these crazy thoughts he'd been having about his assistant, Justin reminded himself. He snatched up his brief-case, retrieved his suit coat and headed toward the exit.

So, he would get a handle on it, he assured himself, as he stepped into the elevator. All he had to do was treat this new attraction he was experiencing toward Kim as he would a business or marketing problem. These next few days away from Kim—tomorrow in New York and then the weekend—would provide him with the perfect oppor-tunity to do just that. Squaring his shoulders, Justin stepped off the elevator and, after signing out with the guard on duty, he headed for the garage.

A few days away from Kim was just what he needed to put things back into their proper perspective. He and Kim made a good working team. No way did he plan to mess that up by giving in to some crazy urges he'd had to kiss her. He'd already figured out it was his own lack of a social life that had triggered this new attraction he'd felt toward Kim. He'd simply force himself to reclaim some time for a social life. Already feeling better, he breathed a sigh of relief as he slid behind the wheel of his Mercedes. With any luck Kim would never find out just how close he'd come to crossing the line, and their relationship would go back to being business as usual.

It was business as usual when he called Kim from New York the next day. Seated in the back seat of the taxi en route to his meeting, Justin listened on his cell phone as Kim relayed his messages.

"Ashley Powers called. She said that you owe her a dinner and she'd like to collect soon."

Justin thought of the striking brunette stockbroker he'd taken out a few times this spring. The woman was beauti-ful, intelligent and had been sending him signals that she was more than ready to take their relationship to the next level. He'd been prepared to take her up on her offer for more than a month now, but their busy schedules kept getting in the way. Maybe Ashley was just what he needed to firmly shut off any lingering attraction he felt for Kim. "What's on my calendar for next Friday night?" Justin paused, and when Kim didn't answer, he asked, "Kim, you still there?"

"Yes. I was just pulling up your calendar on my screen. Right now you're open."

"See if Ashley's free for the evening. If she is, make us dinner reservations. Try that new place mentioned in that food critic's column last week."

"All right," Kim replied.

"What else have you got for me?"

"Robert Marsh said he needs to speak with you."

"What does he want?" Justin asked, agitated that Marsh was the reason he was in New York. Had the other man paid closer attention to the details, he wouldn't be scrambling to clean up a mess now.

"He wouldn't tell me. He said it was personal and had to do with family business."

Justin frowned, disliking the way Marsh had taken to identifying himself as a member of the Connelly family. Perhaps Justin had become jaded, but every instinct in him said Marsh was far more in love with the idea of marrying into the Connellys than he was in love with Alexandra. "Inform Marsh that he can either tell you what it is he wants or he can wait until I get back in the office on Monday."

"I'll tell him."

"Is that it?"

"Not quite. You have two more phone messages. One is from Patrice Barlow, who said to tell you that she and her daughter Bethany will be at the bachelor auction tonight and that Bethany will be making a substantial bid on you.''

Justin groaned aloud. ''Let's hope that her bid's not too substantial. I'm not sure I could handle spending an entire evening with Bethany the debutante.''

''She's not that bad,'' Kim told him.

''Easy for you to say. You've never been trapped at a dinner party with her and forced to listen to her ramble on and on about sororities in that squeaky voice of hers.''

''She's very pretty,'' Kim offered.

''How can you tell under all that makeup? The last time I saw her she was wearing so much gloss on her mouth that I thought the wineglass was going to slip across her lips and she'd end up with wine in her ear.''

''You're making that up!''

''All right, maybe I am exaggerating a little,'' he said. ''But you have to admit, the woman does overdo the makeup.''

''Maybe a little,'' Kim conceded.

He didn't have to see Kim's face to hear the smile in her voice, to imagine the grin curving her lips—lips with just a touch of rose color, and far more inviting than Bethany Barlow's could ever be. Realizing where his thoughts were headed, Justin sobered at once. ''You said I had another message.'' he prompted, reverting to business.

''Yes, from your sister Tara. She just wanted to wish you luck today and to say thanks in advance for agreeing to participate in the auction tonight.''

''In other words, she called to remind me that I'd better show up tonight or I'm toast,'' Justin countered.

''I wouldn't put it that way exactly. She's just a little nervous and wants to make sure there are no glitches.''

''Nice try, Kim. But I know my little sister. She had you double-check the flight arrangements, didn't she?''

Kim hesitated. "I *offered* to check."

Uh-huh, Justin thought. No doubt his sister had made an ally of Kim. Not that he was surprised. People seemed to gravitate toward Kim, and heaven knew that Tara could use a friend after the rough time she'd had these past years. "Tell Tara not to worry. A promise is a promise. I'll be there."

"I'll tell her," Kim replied. After a moment's pause, she said, "That's everything for the moment."

"Good," he said, but found himself reluctant to cut the connection.

"Was there anything else you needed me to do?" Kim asked.

"No. No, you've covered everything as usual."

"Just doing my job," she informed him. "Speaking of which, I better start making those calls."

"Kim, wait."

"Yes?"

"Promise me that you'll get out of there on time for a change. I don't like the idea of you working late alone."

"Justin, I'm perfectly safe. The security—"

"Promise me," he insisted.

"All right. I promise to leave on time. I was going to leave at five today, anyway."

"Big plans for the evening?" The question slipped out before he could stop himself.

"Kind of. I'm going to the fund-raiser tonight at the hotel. Your sister bought extra seats and insisted on giving me a ticket to attend. That is if my being there doesn't make you uncomfortable. If it does, I can tell Tara I can't make it."

"Why would your presence make me uncomfortable?"

"I...don't know. It's just that you've seemed a little

edgy the past few days. I thought that maybe it was me, that I'd done something to make you uncomfortable."

"I'm just uptight about the Schaeffer meeting," Justin lied. "By all means go to the fund-raiser. It'll be nice to see a friendly face there."

"If you're sure..."

"Positive. Come. Bring your boyfriend, and the two of you can have a great time." Before she could reply, he ended the call by saying, "Got to run. I'm at Schaeffer's now. I'll see you tonight."

Kim stared at her reflection in the mirror, unable to believe that the elegant creature who looked back was actually her. She smoothed her hands down the skirt of the strapless black evening gown. And when her gloved fingers whispered along the moiré silk fabric, she fell in love with the dress all over again. Dismissing the last pangs of guilt over splurging on the outfit, Kim smiled. Both the dress and the matching eighteen-button doeskin gloves had been worth every penny, she decided, as she turned to admire the way the skirt swished about her ankles.

The store clerk had been right. It was the type of gown that made a woman feel like a princess. And Kim couldn't help feeling a bit like Cinderella on her way to the ball. Lifting her skirt, she studied the high-heeled shoes with their delicate straps. "Not exactly glass slippers," she murmured.

But every bit as impractical, she thought, and laughed aloud at her own foolish purchase. She'd probably never wear the shoes again. And the likelihood that she'd ever have an occasion to wear the gown and gloves again were just as slim, she admitted. Yet for now, for tonight, it didn't matter. Tonight she could pretend she was a princess attending her first ball.

"Good evening, My Lord," she mimicked. Enjoying the game, she executed a curtsy and giggled when she wobbled on the skyscraper heels. Definitely not walking shoes, she reminded herself, and made a mental note to take small, slow steps tonight. Otherwise, she'd be tumbling in the middle of the ballroom floor in front of all those important people. The idea of disgracing herself that way sent a shudder through Kim. She hugged her arms to herself. She could just imagine what Justin's reaction would be to the sight of her sprawled on the floor.

Justin.

She pressed a palm to her belly to quell the flurry of butterflies set off by thoughts of seeing him tonight. Studying her reflection in the mirror, she couldn't help wonder what he would think when he saw her. Would he think she looked pretty or...?

What on earth was she doing?

Furious with herself for indulging in foolish fantasies, Kim reminded herself that fancy clothes couldn't change who or what she was. It certainly wouldn't alter the way Justin thought of her. She was his dependable, boring assistant, and nothing more. Any notions that Justin might see her in any other light had surely been dispelled that last evening they were alone at the office together, hadn't it?

Shame heated her cheeks as she recalled how she'd gotten the insane idea in her head that Justin was going to kiss her that night. Well, he hadn't, she recalled and felt another sharp jolt of embarrassment. Irritated that the memory of Justin's rejection could still rattle her so, she gave herself a mental shake. Instead of feeling sorry for herself, she should be grateful that Justin hadn't known what she'd been thinking, what she'd been wanting him to do. Another shudder went through her at the idea. It was bad enough that she'd allowed herself to fall in love with Justin Connelly. The only thing worse would be her humiliation if he had discovered that fact. Had he done so, she would never have been able to face him again. Which meant she would have no choice but to resign her position at Connelly Corporation.

Drawing in a calming breath, Kim told herself it was better this way. It was past time that she put to rest the ridiculous idea of a relationship between her and Justin. To do otherwise would surely lead to disaster. She needed only to look at all the heartache her own mother had endured by clinging to such foolish romantic notions. As always was the case when she thought of her mother, Kim felt the pang of loss anew. Despite the fact that she'd often felt their roles had been reversed and that she had assumed the parental responsibility, she still missed her mother terribly. She could only pray that at long last Amanda Lindgren had found the fairy-tale ending that had eluded her in life.

Thank heavens she had been born with a healthy dose of pragmatism, Kim told herself. This was the real world— not some fairy tale. Handsome, multimillionaires like Justin Connelly simply didn't fall in love with their assistants. They fell in love with beautiful models or wealthy debutantes or chic businesswomen who belonged to country clubs and moved in the same social circles. No, when a man like Justin fell in love, it would be with a woman who could trace her ancestors back to the *Mayflower* or who had a royal bloodline like his. Not with the illegitimate daughter of a pretty but flighty file clerk who'd become pregnant before discovering the man who'd professed his love was already married to someone else.

Kim had long since come to terms with who she was, and would be forever thankful that she'd had a mother who'd truly loved and wanted her. While her mother's romantic disasters might have been despairing to watch, it had grounded her and made her all the more determined not to delude herself. She was quiet, reliable Kim Lindgren—not at all the type of woman who would appeal to the likes of Justin Connelly.

Yet as she stared at her reflection in the mirror, Kim found it difficult to reconcile the woman she saw there with the shy woman inside her. The woman in the elegant evening gown didn't resemble mousy Kim at all. She looked as if she actually belonged in Justin's world.

Realizing what she was doing, Kim put a halt to her ridiculous musings and blamed her errant thoughts on the dress. But as she subjected herself to another critical once-over, she frowned. It wasn't just the dress. It was the hair, Kim determined as she eyed the sweep of blond tresses that fell down around her shoulders. Wearing her hair down to cover her bare shoulders had seemed like a good idea at the time. But now she wondered if it had been a mistake. It made her look…sensual, almost sexy.

Which just went to show how deceiving appearances could be, Kim mused. She was practical and level-headed Kim Lindgren, not some sexy femme fatale. And there was no point in sending out false signals. Walking over to the vanity table, she dug out her hairpins and reached for the brush, intent on redoing her hair in its customary twist. But before she'd had time to do more than gather the hair into her fist, the doorbell sounded.

The driver Tara had insisted on sending for her, Kim surmised. The last thing she wanted to do was keep the man or Tara waiting for her. Sighing, she released the rope of blond hair from her fist, and it tumbled back down about her shoulders. The hair would just have to do as it was, she decided. Snatching up her evening bag, she headed for the door.

"Good evening, Miss Lindgren. My name is James."

"Good evening, James."

She allowed the driver to escort her from her apartment building to the sleek, black limousine parked out front. After opening the car door, he took her arm gently and assisted her inside.

"Thank you," she murmured, and slipped inside the vehicle. Despite the fact that she'd worked for the Connellys for two years, she still found herself in awe of the amenities their wealth provided. The dark leather seats looked butter soft. Unable to resist, she swept her gloved fingers along the smooth surface as her gaze flitted over the plush carpeting and tinted windows. There was enough room inside for at least ten people, Kim thought. Amused and delighted, she settled against the cushiony backrest and reached for her seat belt.

Having already resumed his position behind the wheel, James turned to address her. "We should arrive at the hotel in approximately twenty minutes, Miss Lindgren. Mrs. Paige instructed me to tell you to sit back, relax and enjoy the ride. Should you care for a cocktail or something to drink while we're en route to the hotel, you'll find a fully stocked bar to your left."

"Thank you. But I'm fine," Kim told him as she noted the built-in bar he had indicated.

"Very well, ma'am. I'll be closing the privacy window, but if you should need me for anything or have any questions, just press the call button next to your seat."

"Thank you. I'll do that, if I need anything."

James nodded. Within seconds the glass partition separating them slid shut, and moments later the car slipped out into the Friday evening traffic.

From the back of the limousine Kim stared out at the familiar streets and landmarks. But as she watched the city of Chicago transform beneath the shimmer of stars and the glow of the streetlights, Kim could feel the anticipation dancing in her own veins. And if she didn't chill out, she was going to burn out like a shooting star before she ever got to the hotel.

Taking a deep breath she pressed a hand to her midsection in an effort to quell the nerves that were playing havoc with her stomach. It didn't help. Nothing did, she admitted. She simply found it impossible to relax.

But then, who could blame her? Here she was, sitting in the back of a limousine, dressed to the nines and on her way to a black-tie fund-raiser as Tara Connelly Paige's guest.

She might as well enjoy it while she could, Kim decided, since this would probably be her first and last ride in a limo. Oddly enough, that realization and the decision to enjoy herself seemed to settle her nerves somewhat. She was just beginning to relax when the phone rang and she tensed up all over again.

"It's for you, miss," James informed her seconds later as he lowered the privacy panel. His eyes met hers briefly in the rearview mirror. "There's a receiver in the panel directly in front of you."

"Thank you," Kim murmured and reached for the phone. "Hello?"

"Kim, it's Tara. What a relief. I had visions of you changing your mind and canceling on me tonight."

"Well, I did think about it," Kim admitted. In fact, she'd considered begging off several times during the past few days. But then she'd spied the evening gown in a store window yesterday, and when she'd gone inside the boutique and discovered it was her size and on sale to boot, she'd taken it as a sign.

"I'm certainly glad you didn't," Tara told her, and proceeded to recount for Kim the maddening day she'd had.

"As if the problems with the centerpiece weren't enough to deal with, one of our bachelors managed to break his leg while skydiving and wanted to bow out of the auction. Fortunately, Jennifer and I were able to convince him that parading around in a cast would drive up his bidding price."

"And I take it he believed you?"

"Of course," Tara told her with the assurance of a woman who had never accepted the word no from anyone.

"Sounds like you've had quite a day."

"I have. That's why the thought of you canceling on me tonight would have been one problem I simply couldn't have handled."

Surprised, Kim said, "Thanks. But I hardly think one empty seat at a table would make a big difference."

"Actually, it would, since you'll be doing a bit more than just filling a seat."

Kim drew her brows together. "What do you mean?"

"Oh, it's nothing much really," Tara said breezily. "I just need you to do me a little favor, to sort of help out with the auction."

"Help out how?" Kim asked, suddenly uneasy.

"Like I said, it's just a little favor, and it'll keep Justin from wringing my neck. But it's nothing for you to worry about. I'll explain it all to you when you get here."

Warning bells went off. "Tara, about this favor—"

"Don't worry. I'll explain it all to you later."

"But—"

"Oops, got to run," Tara said. "See you in a little bit."

"Tara, wait—"

But it was too late. The dial tone was already buzzing in her ear. And as she hung up the phone, Kim realized her nervous excitement had been replaced by a new emotion— worry.

Four

"**Y**our tuxedo and shoes are in the back seat, Mr. Connelly."

"Thanks, Hal," Justin told the stoic-looking driver who'd met him at O'Hare Airport moments earlier. He reached inside and grabbed the garment bag, intent on changing in the airport men's room.

Hal cleared his throat. "If you'll pardon me, sir. Miss Tara suggested that it might save time if you were to change clothes in the limo while we're en route to the hotel."

"In other words, my sister told you to make sure I don't leave your sight until you deliver me to her cattle auction."

"Not at all, sir," Hal said formally, standing beside the sleek black limo. "Miss Tara merely said I should make the suggestion."

"If you say so," Justin replied, and climbed into the back of the limo. Even as he stripped off his tie and ditched his suit coat, the car pulled away from the curb. Knowing his sister as he did, Justin had no doubt that Tara had batted her violet eyes at the long-time driver and told the man that she was depending on him to get Justin to the fund-raiser on time.

Justin grimaced as he thought of the bachelor auction and wished, yet again, that he hadn't agreed to participate. He still believed a generous check to the charity would have sufficed. But then, he'd always found it difficult to say no to his sister. And then there had been Kim, calmly pointing out how simple it would be for him to keep his promise to attend the event.

Kim.

As happy as he was about salvaging the Schaeffer deal, he was even more pleased that he had been able to put this new attraction to Kim into perspective. Until this thing with Schaeffer had gotten settled, he hadn't realized how consumed he'd been with business during these past few months. Since Kim had been the woman he'd spent most of his time with, it was only natural that he had been drawn to her. That was all it was, he assured himself. Now that he had himself in hand, he could only be grateful that he hadn't given in to the urge that night to kiss her.

Pleased with his assessment of the situation and confident that he had everything under control again, Justin smiled as he reached for the cummerbund. Kim said she would be at the fund-raiser tonight. The fact that he was looking forward to seeing her had nothing to do with his growing attraction to her, he reasoned. It was simply that he knew she'd be as excited as he was about the way the Schaeffer deal had turned out. Slipping the tie around his neck, Justin sat back and thought of the evening ahead.

As much as he disliked the idea of being auctioned off, it really was for a good cause. The fact that it would make

Tara and Jennifer happy made it somewhat more palatable. And, of course, not having to wait until Monday to see Kim's face when he told her about the outcome of the Schaeffer meeting made the evening ahead actually appealing.

Who knew, Justin mused as he gave up on getting the tie right. Maybe tonight wouldn't be so bad after all.

"I feel like a prize steer at a cattle auction," Justin complained thirty minutes later as he waited backstage for the bachelor auction to begin.

"Oh, for heaven's sake, quit bellyaching," Tara countered as she looked him over with a critical eye and zeroed in on the tie he'd managed to mangle. "This is going to be fun."

"Easy for you to say. You're not the one who has to parade around on that stage out there in front of a man-hungry audience."

"And since when do you dislike being the center of attention in a roomful of females?" she asked as she proceeded to redo his tie.

"Since Eve Novak cornered me on my way backstage."

Tara paused. She lifted her gaze to his and arched her brow. "Oh? And what did Evie say to put you into such a foul mood?"

Ignoring the foul-mood accusation, he said, "It's not so much what she said, it's the way she looked at me when she said it."

"And just how did she look at you, big brother?" Tara teased.

"Like a hungry cat that had just cornered its next meal," Justin grumbled. "Now I know what women mean when they complain about a guy undressing them with his eyes.

For a minute there I half expected her to pinch my a—my, uh, butt.''

"I'm sure she thought about it," Tara informed him as she went back to adjusting his tie. "Word at the country club is that Eve's in the market for a new husband."

"I thought she just got married again last year."

"She did. But apparently marriage to a cowboy wasn't what Eve expected. As of last week, she's single again."

"I'll probably kick myself for asking," Justin began, "but what happened?"

"It seems that Mr. Tall, Dark and Texan was under the mistaken impression that Evie was going to ride off into the sunset with him. The poor guy actually thought the two of them were going to have little cowboys and cowgirls of their own and live happily ever after on his ranch."

Poor guy was right, Justin thought. How anyone would believe the self-indulgent, spoiled Eve Novak would even agree to have a child, let alone actually raise one was beyond him. "The guy must have had a little too much cactus juice if he believed that. Eve has never struck me as the maternal type."

"Me, neither," Tara replied. "But then, I suspect it wasn't her maternal instincts that Tex was drawn to in the first place."

His sister was right. Eve Novak was a beautiful and glamorous woman—the kind who always drew a man's eye. But he had never been even slightly interested in her, Justin admitted. Probably because there was something almost predatory about the woman that turned him off. Which was why he'd never even been tempted to follow through on any of the invitations, blatant or otherwise, that she'd cast his way over the years. And he didn't intend to start tonight, either.

"But you shouldn't have anything to worry about where

Eve is concerned,'' Tara told him, and stepped back to survey her handiwork.

Justin narrowed his eyes. "What do you mean?"

"I mean that I doubt Eve has any intention of treating you like a son if she wins you in the auction tonight."

Justin's blood ran cold at his sister's gibe. "You'd better be joking, brat. Because if I thought for one minute that there was a chance I'd get stuck on a date with Eve Novak, I'd be out of here so fast it would make your head spin."

When Tara bit her bottom lip and remained silent, Justin broke out in a sweat. "Tara, tell me that there's no way Eve Novak has any chance of winning me in this auction."

"And just how am I supposed to do that?" she demanded. "It's an auction, Justin. I don't have any control over who bids what. Considering her trust fund and the settlements from her last three divorces, Eve might very well be in a position to outbid everyone else here tonight."

Justin swore.

"Justin," Tara admonished.

"Sorry," he muttered. And he was sorry. Sorry that he'd ever let himself be talked into this stunt—even if it was for charity. His mind raced for a way out of this mess without going back on his word to his sister and to Jennifer.

"Justin, you really aren't going to leave us in the lurch, are you?"

"No," he told her. "But there's no way I'm going to get stuck with that man-eater, either. Give me a minute. I need to figure this out."

"You may want to think fast, big brother. The auction's going to start in about fifteen minutes."

Justin raked a hand through his hair, resisted the urge to loosen his tie as he paced. "I've got it," he told Tara. "*You* bid on me."

"I can't do that. I'm your sister."

"So?"

"So, how would it look for your own sister to win a date with you?"

Desperate, he suggested, "Then have Jennifer do it."

"She's married to Chance," Tara reminded him. "Somehow I doubt that Chance would appreciate having his wife win a date with his brother."

She was right, Justin admitted. He thought of suggesting Kim since she'd said she would be attending. But he immediately rejected the idea. He'd just got his head straight where she was concerned. Having Kim bid on his date package would be asking for trouble. "I'm not getting saddled for an evening with Eve Novak—not even if it is for a good cause."

Tara patted his jaw. "Relax, big brother. You don't know for sure that Eve will bid on you. After all, you're the last bachelor to go on the block. Eve's never been the patient type. She just might decide to go after one of our other bachelor babes."

He certainly hoped so, Justin thought.

"Besides, I have it on good authority that Ashley Powers plans to bid on you tonight. And who knows, maybe Bethany Barlow's mother will decide to buy you for her daughter."

Justin glared at his sister. "You're enjoying this, aren't you?"

Tara laughed. "Of course I am. Consider it payback for all the times you were mean to me when we were kids."

"I was never mean to you."

"What about the time you refused to let me go sailing with you and Mindy Hastings?"

"Mindy and I were on a date," he returned. "No guy in his right mind lets his kid sister tag along on a date."

"See, I told you. You were mean."

"Tara," Justin said, a warning edge to his voice. He took a step toward his sister.

"Oops. Got to run. It's almost time for the auction to start," she said, and after giving him a quick kiss on the cheek, she dashed off.

"And to think I thought tonight wouldn't be so bad," Justin muttered.

"You say something, Connelly?" Brad Parker, one of the other bachelors on the block, asked.

"Yeah. Be grateful you don't have any sisters."

Kim moved about the ballroom and did her best not to gawk. The room resembled something out of a fairy tale, she thought, as she took in the splendor that surrounded her. While she had been mesmerized by the sight of the room itself—from the sweep of windows that looked out over the Chicago night sky to the breathtaking crystal centerpieces bursting with lilies, white roses and sprigs of freesia on each table—it was the people in attendance who fascinated her. They were gorgeous. Both the men and the women. And she couldn't recall ever seeing so many beautiful people in one room at the same time.

All right, where the men were concerned it probably was the tuxedos, Kim conceded. After all, what fellow didn't look good in a tux? But as far as the women went, it was a different story. The outfits ran the gamut from fabulous to outrageous. Each one looked more stunning than the next. Surely every yard of silk and lace, not to mention every sequin and bead, in Chicago had gone into the gowns being worn. And despite the large number of people in attendance, she'd yet to see any two dresses alike.

Kim tightened her gloved fingers around her evening bag and couldn't help but be glad that she had splurged on her own outfit. She was also glad she'd taken time with her appearance. As she began making her way back to her table, she spied Ashley Powers, the stockbroker that Justin had taken out on several occasions. Kim couldn't quite help feeling a slight stab of envy as she looked at the statuesque brunette. The woman was breathtaking. When the other woman tipped her head back in laughter, Kim caught the flash of sapphires and diamonds at her neck and ears. Automatically her hand went to her own bare throat and she became keenly aware of the tiny diamond chips in her ears. That old adage about not being able to turn a sow's ear into a silk purse flashed into her mind. And it sent her stomach plummeting—along with her self-confidence.

She didn't belong here.

It had been ludicrous to think that she would. She shouldn't have come, Kim told herself, feeling suddenly foolish. How on earth had she ever convinced herself that a fancy dress and high heels would make any difference? She was Kim Lindgren, not some society darling. And she needed to get out of here before Justin or anyone else saw her and she made an even bigger fool of herself. Her mind made up, she turned toward the exit intent on escape.

"Kim! Kim, wait!"

Kim wanted to ignore the familiar voice but couldn't. Stopping, she turned around and spied Tara hurrying toward her. Mentally she began to prepare a speech about having a headache.

"Thank goodness I found you. I've been trying to get over to your table for the past thirty minutes," she said as she reached her. "And I— Why Kim, you look absolutely stunning."

Caught off guard by the compliment, Kim faltered. "I, um, thank you," she murmured. "It's the dress. I found it on sale." No sooner were the words out of her mouth than

Kim wanted to snatch them back because they sounded so lame.

Tara smiled. "That makes it even better, then. But trust me, it's not the dress. It's you. Why I had no idea you had such beautiful hair."

Kim felt the color race up her cheeks. "Yes, well, I thought I'd wear it down for a change," she told her, and nearly groaned. Could she possibly sound any more inane?

"And I'm sure every man here—including my brother Justin—will be glad that you did. It looks perfect, Kim. If I didn't like you so much, I'd be pea-green with envy that you were born with such gorgeous hair and I got stuck with this mop."

Kim blinked. "But your hair is beautiful. And it always looks so...so chic."

Tara laughed. She ran a hand through her short, dark tresses. "I'm not sure I'd call this chic as much as convenient."

"It's chic. And it suits you," Kim told her. And it did. Tara Connelly Paige had always reminded her of a young Audrey Hepburn with her dark hair and elegant features, and those violet eyes made her think of Elizabeth Taylor in her youth.

"You're very kind," Tara said, her eyes twinkling with humor. "And I'm going to take shameless advantage of that kindness by asking you to do me that little favor I mentioned earlier."

"Tara, I—"

"Well, if it isn't my future sister-in-law Tara, and looking absolutely gorgeous as usual."

"Hello, Robert," Tara said coolly. "What can I do for you?"

"I just wanted to say hello," he said smoothly, his lips

curving into a smile. "Aren't you going to introduce me to your pretty friend?"

Kim sucked in a breath as she realized Marsh didn't recognize her, and she couldn't help wishing that she had been able to make her escape before running into him.

"You mean you don't recognize Kim?" Tara countered.

Marsh whipped his gaze from her bare shoulders up to her face. "Kim Lindgren?"

"Hello, Robert," Kim managed.

"Good Lord, who'd have thought that underneath those prim suits—"

Tara's eyes narrowed. "Don't stop now, Robert. Who'd have thought under those prim suits what?" she prompted.

"Who'd have thought that our little Kim could look so grown-up. You look lovely," he told her, and took her hand in a courtly gesture that didn't match the covetous look in his eyes.

"Thank you," she said, and tugged her hand free, grateful that the gloves she'd worn had protected her from his touch. There had always been something about Robert Marsh that set her on edge. Tonight even more so.

"Where's Alexandra?" Tara asked.

"She's in the ladies' room," Robert replied, but his eyes remained fixed on Kim, which only made her feel more uncomfortable.

"Since Kim and I were just heading there ourselves, I'll let her know where she can find you." And without waiting for Marsh to respond, Tara linked her arm with Kim's and headed across the room.

"Um, Tara, the ladies' room is in the opposite direction," Kim advised when the other woman continued to march them down the hotel corridor away from the ballroom.

"I know. I didn't really have to go to the ladies' room.

I just wanted to get away from Marsh. I know I should at least try to be nice to the man since he's going to marry my sister. But I swear, every time I'm around the guy and he starts laying on the charm, it's as though a neon sign starts flashing the word *phony* in my head and I can't wait to get away from him.''

Kim could certainly understand, because from the first day she'd met Robert Marsh, he had rubbed her the wrong way. He seemed to have a way of watching her that made her skin crawl.

Tara paused next to a column that was far enough away that they could observe the comings and goings in the main ballroom but were somewhat removed from the din. She met Kim's gaze. ''What do you think of Marsh?''

''I...'' Kim fumbled for an answer, unwilling to tell Tara the truth. ''He's obviously a good businessman or he wouldn't be working at Connelly.''

Tara grinned. ''I keep forgetting what a diplomat you are. I know I'm putting you on the spot, but I'd really like you to be honest with me.''

''Well, I can't say that I'm particularly fond of him, but I think the only opinion that really matters is your sister Alexandra's. If she loves him enough to marry him, she obviously sees something in him that you and I don't.''

Tara frowned and seemed to consider that. ''I guess you're right. I just can't help worrying that she's making a mistake.''

''Maybe. But it's her mistake to make.'' And none of the well-meaning lectures or pleas would be able to prevent Alexandra from making that mistake, Kim concluded. Heaven knows, they'd never worked any of the times she'd tried to dissuade her mother from leaping into a romance that had heartache written all over it.

"How did you get so wise?" Tara asked, her voice teasing.

Kim shrugged. "Probably because I didn't have any sisters or brothers to worry about me."

"Oh, my heavens, speaking of brothers, I nearly forgot. I need you to do me a teensy little favor so that I can get out of the doghouse with Justin."

"What's the favor?" she asked warily.

"I need you to buy Justin in the auction."

"What!"

"You've got to do this for me, Kim. For Justin. He was freaking out backstage when he heard that Eve Novak was here and looking for husband number four. She sort of insinuated to Justin that she intended to bid on him. And now he's threatening to pull out of the auction because he's afraid Eve the man-eater will outbid everyone else and he'll get stuck spending an evening with the woman."

Kim knew who Eve Novak was. And man-eater was an accurate description if even half of the stories she'd heard about the woman were true. But as much as she disliked the idea of Justin with Eve Novak, or anyone else for that matter, there was little she could do about it. "I'm sorry, Tara. But I don't see how I can possibly help you. Maybe you should talk to Ashley Powers or Bethany Barlow. I know they both intend to bid on Justin."

Tara shook her head. "Neither one of them is going to be willing to come up with the kind of bid that will make Eve back off."

And Tara thought that she could? She didn't live in the same world that Tara Connelly Paige did. For that matter, she didn't live in the same world that most of the people attending tonight's gala did. Deciding she needed to be blunt, Kim said, "Even if I wanted to, I couldn't bid on

Justin. I know what kind of money these auctions raise. And I...I simply can't afford it. I'm sorry."

"Oh, Kim, sweetie, I could just kick myself," Tara told her and there was genuine regret in the other woman's eyes. "I never meant that I wanted you to use your own money to bid on Justin. I want you to use mine."

"Yours? But then why—"

"Because how would it look for me to buy a date with my own brother?"

While Kim was still digesting that tidbit, Tara caught her hand and pressed a check into her palm. "That's a cashier's check made out to the Police Association's Fund for Widows and Orphans. Use it to buy Justin in the auction."

"Tara, I don't think—"

"Please," she pleaded when Kim attempted to refuse the check. "Do this as a favor to me. And to Justin."

Still unsure what to do, Kim looked at the check that Tara had closed into her palm. "It's for fifteen thousand dollars."

"I know," Tara said, a mischievous gleam in her violet eyes. "That should help you give Eve a run for her money, don't you think?"

Kim nodded.

"But what happens if I win?"

Tara grinned. "Why, you enjoy your date with Justin, of course. Because something tells me he's certainly going to enjoy his date with you."

"You're wrong," Kim insisted, but looked away for fear Tara would see the truth in her eyes. "Justin's my boss. He and I— It's not that way between us."

"Are you sure? I thought I picked up on something the other day."

"You're mistaken," Kim told her.

"I'm sorry, Kim. But you really don't lie worth beans."

Giving up, Kim asked, "Am I that obvious?"

"Only to someone who remembers what it's like to be in love with someone who doesn't exactly belong to the same social register as you do."

"But you and your family are rich," Kim blurted out.

"But Michael wasn't. I might have been the one with money but that doesn't mean it was easier."

"I guess I never thought of it that way," Kim murmured, knowing that the other woman was referring to her brief marriage to Michael Paige. She thought of how Tara had been declared a widow when her husband's body had failed to turn up following a train derailment two years earlier. "I'm sorry," Kim said, and touched the other woman's arm. "I can't imagine what it's been like for you these past two years."

Tara shrugged. "At least I have my son."

"Yes," Kim replied, recalling the little boy she'd seen with Tara on occasion.

The sound of drum rolls from the ballroom spilled out into the corridor. "Sounds like the auction's about to start. We'd better get inside."

Suddenly nervous again, Kim said, "Tara, about the auction. I'll make the bid, but as for the date, I'd rather you'd let Justin give the package to one of his lady friends."

"But why?"

"Because it would be awkward. We work together and he...doesn't see me that way."

"How do you know, when you're so busy trying to make sure he never sees the real you?"

Five

"All right, ladies, I have thirty-eight hundred dollars for Mr. David Brighton and his gourmet dinner for two, followed by an evening of dancing. Do I hear thirty-nine hundred dollars?" the auctioneer prompted from her position behind the dais on the stage where the bachelors had been marched out like prize cattle for the past forty-five minutes.

"Thirty-eight fifty," a redhead with fawn-colored eyes called out, and waved her numbered paddle enthusiastically.

"I have thirty-eight hundred and fifty dollars. Do I hear thirty-nine hundred?" When no one responded, the auctioneer, milking the crowd for more, said, "Come on, ladies. Remember this is for charity. And Mr. Brighton here is offering a five-course gourmet meal and an evening of dancing at one of Chicago's hot new nightspots for the lucky lady with the winning bid."

"All right, thirty-nine hundred dollars," a sulky-mouthed

brunette declared and immediately shot a menacing glance to the redhead at the next table who had started to raise her paddle. "And don't you dare top my bid, Sarah Hartley."

"I wasn't going to," Sarah replied, and tipped her nose up.

The auctioneer, evidently realizing the bidding war was over said, "Going once. Going twice. Going three times. Sold," she pronounced with a bang of her gavel. "To Ms. Candace Larson for thirty-nine hundred dollars."

From his position backstage, Justin watched Brighton strut offstage to be claimed. Turning away, he tuned out the next bachelor being put on the block and resigned himself to the fact that he was next. He reminded himself that it was for a good cause and tried not to think that he would much rather have gone to the office and tackled some paperwork.

Thinking of the office made him think of Kim again. He hadn't seen her as yet—at least, she hadn't been seated at Tara's table. Nor had he spotted her when he'd scanned the crowd. Had she changed her mind about coming? he wondered. Surprised at how disappointed that idea made him, Justin assured himself he was simply anxious to tell Kim about the Schaeffer meeting. After all, he reasoned, she'd worked as hard as he had to put it back together.

Lost in thought, he didn't even realize the emcee had given the signal for him to come out onstage until the hotel liaison assigned backstage for the event cleared his throat and said, "Mr. Connelly, sir, that's your cue."

Justin jerked his gaze to the young man. "Um, thanks," he said, and bracing himself, he walked out on stage.

"Our final bachelor up for bid tonight is Mr. Justin Connelly."

Justin walked out onto the stage and managed what he

hoped would pass as a happy-to-be-there smile while cameras flashed, party-goers clapped and one or two unladylike whistles rang out. Between the stage lights and camera flashes, it took Justin a moment to adjust his eyes. Once he did, he began to scan the sea of faces as he moved down the length of the stage.

"The vice president of marketing for the Connelly Corporation, Justin is a member of one of Chicago's finest families and the brother of the recently crowned king of Altaria. A familiar face on the business, civic and social scene, he was recently voted one of the most eligible bachelors in Chicago."

Ignoring the catcalls that followed that little tidbit, Justin shoved his hand into his pocket and started back toward the center of the stage. As he did so, he couldn't help feeling a whole new level of respect for the women who participated in beauty pageants. He knew many of them did so for scholarship money or a break in show biz. And all he could think now was how on earth did they handle this sort of thing?

"Now, let's see what special date Justin is offering our bidders." Smiling, the emcee untied the ribbon around the envelope that held a certificate describing his date package. After adjusting her spectacles, the woman practically beamed when she said, "Ladies, all I can say is get out your checkbooks."

Evidently Kim had managed to secure tickets for some hot new show, Justin thought as he approached his mark at the center of the stage. And he couldn't help but wish it were Kim he'd be taking to dinner and the theater. But even as the thought formed, he quashed it.

"You'd also better get out your suntan lotion and bathing suits because some lucky lady is going to spend the day sailing Lake Geneva with Justin aboard his boat *Calypso*.

Then you'll be treated to a catered lunch followed by cocktails at sunset. Now, who's going to get the ball rolling with an opening bid of one thousand dollars?''

Stunned to discover just what Kim had put together as a date package for him, Justin silently vowed to wring his assistant's pretty neck. As much as he loved sailing, he hadn't been on his boat in months because of work. He certainly hadn't realized that Kim even knew about his passion for sailing. One thing was for sure. He positively didn't want to spend an entire day on his boat with some debutante or, even worse, Eve Novak by his side. The idea that he might have to had acid churning in his gut. What in the devil had caused Kim to do such a thing? he wondered. Just as quickly, he admitted it was his own fault. He should have looked at the certificate when Kim had offered. Lost in thought and trying to figure out how he was going to get out of this mess, Justin didn't even realize the bidding was moving fast and furiously until he heard someone say eight thousand.

Eight thousand? Justin yanked his attention to the emcee at the podium.

"I have eight thousand dollars from Ms. Eve Novak. Do I hear eighty-five hundred?" the woman asked.

"Eighty-five hundred."

Justin jerked his gaze back to the audience, and to his left he noted Ashley Powers. He tried to manage a smile of gratitude to the stockbroker, whom he had convinced himself to pursue romantically only a few days earlier,.

"I have eighty-five hundred. Do I hear nine thousand?" The auctioneer asked hopefully. "Ah, I have nine from the lovely young lady in the back."

Justin shifted his gaze toward the rear of the room, tried to see the face of the woman holding paddle number twenty-three. But between the paddle and the persons seated at the front of her table, all he could make out was that she was a blonde.

"Ten thousand," Eve Novak said, drawing his attention back to the front of the room.

"I have ten thousand dollars from Ms. Novak. Do I have—"

"Eleven thousand," Ashley Powers offered from the opposite end of the stage.

"Twelve thousand," Eve countered.

"The bid is at twelve thousand. Do I hear—"

"Fifteen thousand," the blonde in the back called out.

Justin narrowed his eyes and stared at the back of the room. He knew that voice. He was sure of it. And there was something familiar about her. But try as he might, he couldn't quite place the voice or the woman. The brief glimpse he'd gotten of slender shoulders bared by the strapless black dress also drew a blank. No way would he forget a woman with a figure like that. Yet...

"I have fifteen thousand dollars. Do I hear more?" the auctioneer asked, and looked directly at Eve.

"Hey, Justin, you offering more than a boat ride and a sunset?" one of his male friends teased.

"Just my company, Mick."

When the laughter settled down, the auctioneer repeated, "Do I hear more?"

Eve Novak shook her head. Lifting her flute of champagne in a toast, she looked directly at him. "Sorry, Justin honey, but no sailboat ride is worth that kind of money."

"Evidently not everyone agrees," a female voice called out that sounded suspiciously like his sister Tara's, and the room broke out into laughter again.

"All right. Going once. Going twice. Gone." The emcee slammed the gavel down and said, "Sold for fifteen thousand dollars to the owner of paddle number twenty-three.

That concludes our bachelor auction. Thank you, ladies and gentlemen, for your generosity. Enjoy the rest of the evening.''

Relieved to be off the auction block, Justin exited the stage, intent on finding out who the mystery blonde was who'd just paid an extraordinary sum for a date with him. But he'd barely taken two steps when Eve Novak blocked his path.

''Justin.'' She all but purred his name. ''You can't imagine how disappointed I am. I was so counting on having the winning bid for your little sailing date. But even for charity, fifteen thousand dollars seemed awfully high.''

''Yeah, it was a surprise to me, too,'' Justin said, and tried to look past Eve to where the blonde had been seated. Much to his disappointment she was already gone.

''Is she a special friend of yours?''

''Who?'' Justin replied, and only then became aware of how close Eve was standing to him.

''The skinny blonde who just bought the date with you,'' she replied sweetly. But there was no mistaking the hard look in her eyes.

From what little he'd been able to see, his mystery lady might have been on the slender side, but the body in that black number hadn't fit his definition of skinny. ''Actually, I'm not sure.''

''Really? How interesting,'' Eve replied, and Justin felt a prickle of unease snake down his spine at the smile she gave him. She traced one red-tipped nail along his jaw. ''Then perhaps I can convince you to take me out for a spin on your boat even if I didn't win the auction.''

''Now, Eve, how would it look if my brother were to turn around and offer to take all the losing bidders out on his sailboat when someone just paid all that money for the privilege?''

Justin could have kissed Tara for coming to his rescue. Judging from the way her violet eyes sparkled, she knew it, too.

"Hello, Tara," Eve said and there was no mistaking her displeasure at the interruption. "What a surprise seeing you here."

"I don't see why, since both my mother and my brother Chance's wife, Jennifer, are on the fund-raising committee."

"I know. One of the main reasons I came tonight was to support them. And, of course, because your handsome brother here was one of the bachelors being auctioned off." Eve gave Justin a look that smoldered before turning her focus back to Tara. "It's just that when I called this week asking for you to redecorate my apartment, I had the impression you were backlogged. At least, I assumed that's the reason you referred me to an associate."

His sister didn't so much as blink an eye at the underlying accusation in Eve's tone. She simply said, "Business has certainly kept me hopping lately. So has my son. But this fund-raiser is important to my family. Naturally, I made time for it."

"Perhaps you could make time for me as well," Eve suggested.

"Not unless you're willing to wait a few months, until I'm free."

"A few months?" Eve repeated.

"Afraid so. Apparently, my services are in demand at the moment," Tara said smoothly.

Half listening, Justin scoped out the ballroom and spied his mystery blonde walking toward the area designated for tickets and pledges. "Speaking of being in demand," Justin said to Eve and flashed her his most charming smile. "I'm afraid you'll have to excuse me. I just saw my father, and there's something I need to discuss with him.''

Before Eve Novak could object, Justin stepped back and made an immediate bee-line in the direction he'd seen the blonde heading.

''That certainly was an exciting finish for the bachelor auction,'' the woman who'd introduced herself as Linda told Kim as they stood in line with the other winning bidders to settle up their accounts.

''It was exciting for me, too,'' Kim told her. Which was true. It had been exciting and terrifying at the same time. She still couldn't believe she had just shouted out that final bid of $15,000.00. But she'd been so nervous. Then when that sexy blonde in the red dress kept topping the bids for Justin and the people began looking from the blonde to her, she'd only become more nervous. She hadn't been sure she could handle any more rounds of volleying bids and scrutiny, so she'd simply thrown out her top bid, hoping to be done with it.

And she'd won.

''Personally,'' Linda told her, lowering her voice and leaning slightly closer, ''I'm glad you beat that snooty Eve Novak.''

Kim paused, suddenly realizing why the woman seemed familiar. She'd seen her in the society section of the local newspaper and remembered her calling the office for Justin. ''Why?'' Kim asked, curious as to the woman's reason for the comment.

''Because the woman's a real gold digger. She dated the brother of a friend of mine who's an investment banker, but when she found out his own portfolio was modest, she dumped him. Rumor is that she runs D&B checks on all the men she goes out with, and I believe it. Especially considering that all her ex-husbands are millionaires.''

''All?''

''She just got divorced from husband number three,'' Linda explained. ''And since she's here, one can only assume she's on the hunt again. I'm sure she would have just loved the chance to get her hooks into someone with Justin Connelly's money and connections.''

Not sure what to say and feeling guilty for listening to the gossip, Kim remained silent.

''Anyway, congratulations again.''

''Thanks,'' Kim murmured. She was grateful when the line began to move, distracting Linda from discussing Eve Novak or Justin further.

By the time she'd handed over the cashier's check that Tara had given her and was awaiting her receipt, Kim was enjoying herself.

''Here's your receipt and the certificate,'' the woman manning the table told her. ''Enjoy your date.''

''Thank you,'' Kim replied. She turned to leave, only to run into Robert Marsh.

''My, my, you certainly are full of surprises tonight,'' Marsh told her. All the enjoyment of the evening suddenly faded beneath his blatant once-over.

''Excuse me,'' she said, but Marsh blocked her path.

''I just wanted to add my congratulations. That was quite a show you put on during the auction. Justin must be paying you very well if you can afford to spend fifteen grand for a date with him. Or maybe you consider it an investment.''

Kim narrowed her eyes. ''What's that supposed to mean?''

He shrugged and flashed her a smile that did nothing to reassure her. ''Just that I hadn't figured you for someone with designs on snaring her boss.''

"I'm not," Kim informed him, bristling at the implication.

"I certainly hope not because, to be honest, you're not Justin's type. He's into blue-blooded beauties, if you know what I mean."

She did know what he meant, but refused to give him the satisfaction of seeing that his arrow had hit home. "Is there a point to this conversation, Marsh?"

He smiled again. "Just trying to be a friend and offering you the benefit of my experience with the Connellys. I mean, they're a breed unto themselves. Whereas you and I..."

Kim backed away before he could finish his sentence. "Thanks, but I'm afraid you've got the wrong idea. My bidding on Justin tonight was a favor to a friend. Nothing more. Now if you'll excuse me, I just spotted someone that I need to speak with."

Before Marsh could object, Kim dashed past him. She was so intent on getting away that she was scarcely aware the lights had been dimmed and music was now playing. Or that a great many people were making their way to the dance floor. She spied Tara being escorted to the dance floor by an older gentleman, and though she knew she shouldn't intrude, she rushed over to her. "Excuse me, please," she told the man who obviously was surprised by her interruption. Ignoring his arched eyebrow, she shifted her attention to Tara. "I just wanted to thank you again for inviting me tonight."

"I'm the one who should be thanking you," Tara replied, but it was obvious from her expression she didn't understand why Kim was so distressed. "I'm glad that you decided to come."

"Well, it was fun, but I'm going home now and I wanted to say good-night."

"But the evening's just getting started, and—"

"I know. But I'm afraid I do have to go," Kim told her.

"But you can't possibly leave now," a male voice said from behind her, causing Kim's heart to stutter as she recognized the voice. "Not when I've finally tracked down the mystery lady who bought me."

Seeing no way out, Kim dragged in a breath and turned to face him. "I hate to disappoint you but I'm no mystery lady."

"Kim!"

"Afraid so." Her heart sank at the shock she read in Justin's eyes. "I'm sorry. I thought you'd recognized me." Or she had hoped he had, since he'd been looking directly at her when she'd made that final bid.

"I thought…I mean, I knew you seemed familiar, but with the lighting and your hair like that, I didn't realize it was you."

Self-conscious, Kim caught a lock of hair that fell across her shoulder. "I probably should have worn it up."

"No," he said emphatically, surprising Kim. "I like it. You look wonderful."

"I hate to interrupt such an interesting conversation," Tara began, and by her expression, it was clear she wasn't sorry at all. "But in case you haven't noticed, the two of you are standing in the middle of the dance floor. A dance floor that I might add is getting a little crowded."

"Watch out," Justin advised and pulled Kim out of harm's way as an enthusiastic pair nearly collided with her.

"Thanks," Kim murmured, and steadied herself on the sky-high heels, but not before she caught the "I told you so" look from Tara.

"Tara?" the older gentleman who had been standing beside Tara touched her arm. "Shall we?"

"By all means," she replied. Turning her attention back

to the two of them for a moment, she looked straight at her brother and said, "If you can manage to talk and dance at the same time, I suggest you ask Kim to dance."

"Brat," Justin responded, but there was only affection in his eyes as he looked at his sister.

Tara gave him a cheeky smile. "Oh, and no need to thank me now, big brother. You can tell me later how wonderful I am."

"Thank her for what?" Justin asked Kim as Tara danced away.

"For having me buy your date package."

"Tara was responsible?"

Kim nodded. "Maybe we'd better go find someplace where we can talk."

By the time Justin had gotten them each a glass of wine and they had retreated to a relatively quiet corner, Kim had explained how Tara had asked her to attend and bid on him in the bachelor auction. "Anyway, Tara thought you'd prefer to choose your own date and not get stuck with someone because of the auction. So I agreed to bid on you at her request."

"Remind me to send my sister flowers on Monday," Justin told her.

"Then you're not upset?"

"Hardly. I will admit that at first I was ready to strangle you when I discovered that instead of dinner and theater tickets, you'd locked me into an all-day sailing date. Especially when I thought I might have to spend it trapped on the boat with Eve Novak."

"And now?"

"Now I'm looking forward to it," he told her. "But I am curious about something."

"What?"

"How did you know I had a passion for sailing?"

"Oh, that was easy," Kim explained. "You keep a picture in your office of you and some friends on a sailboat. And I remember when your mother was in the office a month or so ago, complaining that you were working too hard. She mentioned something about you not even taking your sailboat out anymore."

"And naturally, you remembered," he said, and the smile he gave made her insides melt.

"Yes." What would he say if he knew that there was little about him that she didn't remember? The way his hair had a tendency to curl at his nape. The way he absently fingered his pen and paced when he was trying to figure out a problem. The way he always removed the pickles from his sandwiches and ate them separately as though they were a treat.

"Then I guess it's a good thing for Connelly Corporation that you're not an industrial spy, because you'd know all our secrets."

"I don't think you have to worry about that. I love my job." And you, she added silently.

"The corporation is lucky to have you. So am I," he told her, and smiled at her once more. "Thanks again for coming to my rescue tonight."

"You're welcome." Setting down her wineglass, Kim retrieved the envelope that contained the certificate that entitled the bearer to a sailing date with Justin and offered it to him. "Here you go. I hope you have a wonderful time."

Justin glanced at the envelope she held out to him, but made no attempt to take it. The look he gave her was filled with confusion and what Kim wanted to believe was disappointment. "Don't *you* want to go with me?"

Kim's heartbeat quickened. She looked away, stared down at her hands, afraid what Justin might read in her eyes. "Well, I just assumed...that is, I thought you would want to ask someone else, maybe Ashley Powers,'' she offered, recalling that he had had her book a dinner reservation for the two of them. "You know, somebody whose company you enjoyed."

Justin tipped her chin up, and her pulse leaped at the warmth in his hazel eyes. "I enjoy your company, Kim Lindgren, and I can't think of anyone I'd rather take sailing than you. But if you'd rather not go—"

"No. I'd love to go," Kim said, the words tumbling out before she could stop them. "I mean, I've never been sailing before, but I love the water."

"Then it's settled. The two of us have a date to go sailing."

"Well, if you're sure..."

"In the time we've worked together, have you ever known me to be unsure of what I want?"

"No," she conceded. It was one of the things she admired about Justin. He didn't flinch or waver from making decisions.

"In fact, suddenly I can't wait to get out on the water. What do you say we go tomorrow?"

"Tomorrow?"

Justin grimaced. "Already have plans, huh? I should have realized that. All right, we'll just pick another day."

"I don't have plans," she told him. "It's just that I thought...I assumed since you've been out of town, you'd be going to the office tomorrow."

"The office will still be there on Monday, won't it?"

"Well, yes, but—"

"Then, it's settled. Tomorrow you and I are going sailing. All right?"

"All right," she told him, more pleased than he could imagine.

"But seeing how the night's still young, what do you

say we take advantage of the music?'' He stood and held out his hands to her. ''Dance with me?''

''I'm afraid I'm not a very good dancer,'' she told him as the band segued into a cha-cha. She noted the couples on the floor beginning to move in unison. Suddenly she wished she had gone to one of those tony schools that taught young ladies how to ballroom dance.

''I find that hard to believe,'' Justin told her as he drew her to her feet and led her to the dance floor. ''I've yet to discover anything that you don't do well. Besides, I distinctly remember watching you doing those stretching movements not very long ago. The way you moved, I could have sworn you heard music in your head.''

''I did. Well sort of,'' she said, in explanation. ''I exercise to a CD at home, so whenever I do stretches, the music plays in my head. I guess it's a reflex action,'' she continued, only to think what an idiot she must sound like rambling on this way.

But then she couldn't think at all as Justin pulled her into his arms. They were so close she could feel the heat of his body, the warmth of his hand at her back, the way his other palm engulfed her own. She could smell that woods and outdoor scent that she always associated with him. And she could see the flecks of gold in his eyes as he looked down at her.

''Relax and listen to the music,'' he told her.

But as he began to move them about the floor, she couldn't relax. She could barely hear anything, either, save for the frantic beat of her own heart that echoed in her ears.

As though sensing her feelings, Justin pressed her hand against his chest and asked, ''Feel that? Thump-thump, thump-thump, thump-thump.''

''Yes,'' she whispered.

''The music has the same beat. Just like my heart. Thump-thump. Thump-thump. Thump-thump.''

And suddenly she felt it. That same thump-thump sound. Or maybe it was Justin's heartbeat she felt, heard in her head. She wasn't sure. All she knew was that when he slid his hand to her hip and began to lead her into the dance, her body moved in tandem with his. His eyes never left hers, nor did her eyes leave his. Even when the tempo increased, when thigh brushed against thigh, when his hand tightened on her hip, when he spun her around. Each time, she stayed with him, followed his lead, felt the beat of the music, the beat of Justin's heart.

By the time the song finally ended and Justin pulled her against him, her own heart was beating in tune with his. It was as if there was no one else in the world but the two of them.

His eyes flashed with heat, and anticipation shot through her like a rocket as his head began to lower. ''Kim.'' He whispered her name.

''Justin, my man, I've been looking for you.''

Kim jolted at the sound of Robert Marsh's voice. Instinctively she took a step back and crossed her arms.

''Marsh.'' Justin acknowledged the other man with a curt greeting.

''I was wondering how your meeting with Schaeffer went?''

''My meeting went fine.''

''Great, did he—''

''We'll discuss it on Monday,'' Justin said, his voice and expression hard. ''Now if you'll excuse us, I want to tell Jennifer what a great job she did on the fund-raiser.''

''I'm glad things went well in New York. I meant to ask you about it,'' Kim told him. ''But with the excitement of the auction I guess I forgot.''

He smiled at her, and Kim's stomach quivered. "You're not the only one. I was just as eager to tell you how well the meeting went, but I'm afraid business has been the last thing on my mind tonight."

Kim tried not to read anything into what he said, but she was finding it more and more difficult not to do so. "Yes, well. I'll look forward to hearing all about it on Monday."

The music started up again, this time a slow, haunting love song. "Shall we?"

Kim hesitated. "I really should go."

"Don't," he said, stroking her cheek with the back of his hand. "Stay."

She stayed.

And by the time Justin had insisted on accompanying her home, Kim had to pinch herself to be sure she wasn't dreaming. Suddenly the back of the limo that had seemed so large en route to the gala seemed small with Justin seated beside her. In the dim interior, there was something so intimate in the sight of his leg next to hers, of his shoulder just grazing hers, of his arm draped along the back of the seat. Lost in thought, she didn't even realize the car had stopped until the driver was opening her door.

"I'll only be a few minutes," Justin informed the chauffeur as he led Kim to her apartment building.

"Justin, you don't have to walk me up. I'll be fine."

He leveled a reproachful look at her. "And risk my mother's wrath for not seeing a young lady to her door? Never."

"Your mother would never know unless you told her," Kim informed him even as they started up the stairs.

"I'd know."

"This is it," she said, standing outside her apartment.

Justin took the key from her, unlocked the door. "I had a great time tonight," he told her.

"So did I," she murmured, and wished the night didn't have to end. Feeling awkward, unsure what to do, she pasted a bright smile on her face. "Well, I guess I'll see you in the morning. Good night."

"Kim, aren't you forgetting something?"

Confused, Kim squinched her brows together, looked at Justin's face, then down at her apartment key in his outstretched hand. "Oh," she said, feeling like an idiot and reached for the key.

Justin closed his fingers around her hand and pulled her toward him. "I wasn't talking about the key. I was talking about this," he told her just before his mouth touched hers.

His lips moved over hers tentatively at first, as though he were testing, tasting, coaxing. His gentleness disarmed her. And when his tongue traced the seam of her mouth, Kim's lips parted instinctively. He made some sound deep in his throat, part groan, part moan that sent a trill of excitement skating up her spine.

He still held her hand between them, but with his free arm he pulled her against him, and the feel of his arousal pressed against her unleashed a wave of longing inside her. His tongue thrust into her mouth, parried with her tongue, engaged in a mating dance as old as time. Heat arrowed through her belly, between her thighs. And when Kim was sure that she would die if he didn't make love to her in the next five minutes, Justin pulled back.

It took her a moment to register his hot and thunderous expression. "Justin?"

"I'll see you in the morning. Nine o'clock okay?"

"Yes," she replied.

"Great."

He bolted and was halfway down the stairs before she'd had a chance to ask him what was wrong.

Six

So they'd both had a little too much wine to drink last night and had kissed. It was no big deal, Justin reassured himself the next morning as he exited the Loop and headed for Kim's apartment. Given the circumstances and the tenor of the evening, kissing her good-night had been the natural thing to do.

And if the feel of Kim in his arms, the taste of her mouth beneath his own, had shaken him with the force of an earthquake and kept him awake half the night, then it was to be expected. After all, he was a healthy, red-blooded male whose lack of a social life of late had resulted in a long bout of celibacy. Besides, the sight of Kim in that strapless number with those skinny high heels and all that blond hair tumbling down her back would have tempted even a saint.

He'd never claimed to be a saint.

But he did consider himself honorable. Which was why he'd hightailed it out of there last night before he'd followed through on his instinct to make wild, passionate love to her. Kim was his assistant and his friend, Justin reminded himself as he wheeled his Jeep onto Kim's street. He'd use the sailing outing today to reestablish those boundaries of friendship and squash any lingering lustful thoughts he'd been harboring about his assistant.

Feeling better, he pulled his Jeep up to the curb in front of Kim's building, then hopped out and climbed the stairs to her apartment. He rapped on her door and she answered almost at once.

"Good morning," she said.

The smile she gave him hit him square in the solar plexus, and all he could do was stand there and stare.

She glanced down at her clothes, then back up at him. "Am I dressed wrong?" she asked, her smile dimming.

"No. You look perfect." She looked better than perfect. She looked downright delectable, he admitted. The navy-and-white-striped T-shirt emphasized the curves that he'd glimpsed last night and had tried his best to forget. The white shorts revealed a pair of long, slender legs that her sedate suits and slacks had only hinted at, and triggered his most erotic fantasies. So much for his notion of seeing Kim as only his assistant and friend. It simply wasn't going to happen. The only question was what did Kim want? Had he read more into Kim's response to his kiss last night than had been there?

"Is everything okay?"

"Everything's fine," he assured her. "You all set for your first sailing lesson?"

"All set," she said with a grin, and reached for the tote bag sitting next to the door.

"I'll take that." His hand brushed hers as they both reached for the bag. There was no mistaking the spark that shot through him at the innocent touch. And judging by the way those blue-green eyes of hers had widened, he wasn't the only one who'd felt it.

"I wasn't quite sure what I should bring," she informed him as she locked the door.

"Sunscreen?" he asked, lifting the tote bag.

"Yes. Plus a visor, towel and swimsuit."

"Then we're in business," he told her, and followed her down the stairs and out to the street. "All set?" he asked after he'd stowed her tote bag and they'd both buckled their seat belts.

"All set."

He started the Jeep's engine. "Then sit back, relax and enjoy the ride."

They both enjoyed the ride, Justin admitted ninety minutes later as he and Kim set off from the docks of the yacht harbor and headed for the open waters of Lake Geneva. The conversation during the drive had been spirited and fun, with an edge of excitement that he could only attribute to the sexual tension that hummed between them. With an eagerness that he dared not examine too closely, he'd wasted no time loading Kim's tote bag and the picnic-basket lunch he'd picked up at a gourmet deli en route to the lake.

"Are you sure there's nothing I can do to help?" Kim asked him from her position at the bow.

"Don't worry, I intend to make you work for your lunch, sailor. But not until we get past the bend in the harbor and away from the docks."

"All right," she told him, a smile spreading across her lips before she turned away and looked out to the open water.

Mindful to keep his attention on the operation of the sailboat and not Kim's long legs, Justin maneuvered the thirty-five-foot beauty around the final bend and into the mouth of the lake. "Okay, sailor," he said as he cut the engine. "Ready for your first lesson?"

"Aye, aye, captain," she said, and gave him a sassy salute. "What do you want me to do?"

"Now, that's a loaded question if I ever heard one," he teased.

She gave him a reproachful look. "I meant what do you want me to do to help with the boat."

"How about coming over here and manning the wheel while I hoist the sails?"

"You want me to drive the boat?"

"Actually, I want you to keep her steady while I run up the jib and mainsail." After a brief explanation, during which time he did his best not to notice just how silky her skin felt or how her hair smelled of apples and sunshine, he asked, "Got it?"

"I think so," she told him. "But promise you'll teach me how to work the sails, too?"

"I promise," he told her.

More than two hours later, when they anchored the boat in a relatively quiet spot on the lake, he taught her the difference between the mainsail and the jib, explained the workings of the boom and masthead, the keel and rudder while they feasted on lunch.

Justin shaved off a chunk of pepper-jack cheese with his knife, and as he ate it he studied Kim. Stretched out on the foredeck, with the breeze from the lake fingering the hair that she'd pulled up into a ponytail, Kim looked even more tempting now than she had last night in that knockout black dress. If she'd been wearing any makeup other than lip gloss and sunscreen, he hadn't been able to tell it. The few hours they'd spent in the sun had put a healthy shot of color in her cheeks. He grinned as he noted a tiny sprinkling of freckles across her nose. She bit into a grape, and Justin's mouth watered as she licked the juice from her lips. He couldn't help remembering how sweet those lips had tasted last night when he'd kissed her.

"How old were you when you first started sailing?" Kim asked, breaking into his none-too-appropriate thoughts.

"Probably right around the time I got potty trained," Justin admitted. "At least that's when my dad started taking me out with him. When I was growing up, my family spent a lot of time at the lake cottage, especially during the summers. Anyway, my dad used to like to go out on the sailboat in the mornings just when the sun was coming up. I've always been an early riser, so he'd let me tag along."

"I'll bet he enjoyed your company."

"Maybe some of the time," Justin conceded, even though he had always considered those mornings a special bonding time between him and his father. "My dad claimed the lake was a good place for a man to go when he needed to think or when life seemed to be too much. He said being on the lake helped a body to remember that there are more important things in life than making money or building empires."

"I can see why your father is so successful. He's a very wise man."

"Yes, he is." Reminiscing about those quiet mornings he'd spent with his father, Justin realized just how wise a man Grant Connelly had been—even back then. He himself, on the other hand, had not been nearly as wise, Justin decided, as he thought of how consumed with work he'd been these past six months.

"Why the name *Calypso?*" Kim asked, referring to the sailboat's name.

Justin smiled and shook off his deep thoughts. "It's after the sea nymph."

"The one who detained Odysseus on the island of Ogygia for seven years?"

"One and the same," Justin said, impressed that she remembered the tale. "The minute I saw her, I fell under her spell and knew I had to have her. I didn't even haggle about the price. I just wrote out the check."

"Somehow I don't think you have any regrets."

"I don't," he admitted. "At least not about buying the boat. I do, however, regret that it took my very wise assistant putting together a date package for a bachelor auction to get me to come out on her again."

She shrugged and the smile she gave him was filled with sass. "We very wise assistants do what we have to, to keep our bosses from working themselves to death."

"Have I really been that bad?"

"Worse," she told him, and burst into laughter.

"You should do that more often," Justin said.

"What? Book sailing dates with you to be auctioned off for charity?"

"Funny," he said, and pitched a grape at her, which she caught and promptly popped into her mouth. "I meant you should laugh more often. You have a beautiful laugh, Kim."

"Thanks," she murmured and lowered her eyes. She began to toy with the bunch of grapes.

Justin reached over, tipped up her chin. "I didn't mean to embarrass you."

"You didn't," she said, then sighed. "I guess I'm just not used to all this."

"What? Eating lunch?"

She made a face at him. "You know that's not what I meant."

"No? Then you must be talking about sailing. Wait, now

I remember. You did mention something about being a land lover, didn't you?'' he teased.

"I said that I loved the water, and this is the first time I've ever been sailing.''

"Then what is it you're not used to, Kimberly Lindgren? You can't make me believe that before now you haven't had men telling you how beautiful you are.''

"I haven't,'' she whispered so softly that Justin wasn't sure if he heard the words or read the movement of her lips.

"Then the men in Chicago must be blind or mute or both, because you are beautiful, Kim. Incredibly beautiful,'' he told her. Unable to resist, he pressed his mouth against hers.

He took his time. First he kissed the corner of her mouth, slowly savoring the feel of her lips. He lost his fingers in her hair, held her head in his hands while he tested, shaped, explored her mouth. All the while desire burned inside him, spreading like fire, making him hard, making him ache to lose himself in her softness.

Kim's fingers dug into his shoulders, and the sharp bite of her nails served only to feed the fierce hunger churning inside him. But he held himself in check, determined to let Kim set the pace. "Justin,'' she sighed against his lips.

When she opened her mouth to him, his control slipped a notch. He wanted to drink her in and because he did, he forced himself to slow down. She tasted of grapes and lemonade. Of sunshine and sweetness. Of innocence and seduction. She tasted of everything he'd ever wanted and needed in this world, Justin thought. Suddenly he forgot all about the fact that they were anchored in Lake Geneva. That it was the middle of the day and the sun was still shining in the sky. That they were out in the open where anyone and everyone could see them. He forgot about everything but the taste and the feel of the woman in his arms.

Slowly she pulled back, stared up at him out of blue-green eyes shimmering with desire and Justin lost the last of his control. He no longer cared where they were or who saw them. He no longer cared that he'd told himself just last night that this wasn't a good idea. All that mattered now was Kim and the way she was looking at him—as if she wanted him and needed him as much as he wanted and needed her.

Angling his head, he took her mouth again. This time he gave in to the desire that had been driving him mad for weeks. This time he kissed her deeply, thoroughly, with all the hunger inside him that he'd fought to deny. And she kissed him back. Never before had anything felt so right, Justin thought. Never before had he wanted a woman so much. As though sensing his thoughts, she made some mewling sound and pressed herself closer to him.

Justin took the kiss even deeper. He drank in her gasps, mated with her tongue, showed her with his mouth what he wanted to do to her with his body. What he wanted her to do to him with hers. He slid his hands down her back, around her waist, then cupped her breasts.

She tore her mouth free and arched her back, giving him access. While he kissed her neck, he kneaded her breasts. He moved his mouth lower, tasting her collarbone. Then he closed his mouth over one breast, suckled her through her T-shirt and bra. When he closed his teeth on her nipple, she gasped.

"Justin, I—"

The blare from a boat horn drowned out her words as Justin blocked her from view with his body. He glared at the waving passengers on the pleasure craft as they sped by, causing *Calypso* to rock in its wake.

When he looked at Kim again, her cheeks were pink and her eyes were wide with what he suspected was shock. "You okay?" he asked, more gruffly than he'd intended. He still couldn't believe he'd subjected her to the speculation of the idiots in the other boats.

"I'm fine," she told him.

Noting her blouse was still damp from his mouth, he frowned. Evidently she caught the direction of his gaze and crossed her arms over her chest. "I'm sorry," he told her.

"Nothing to be sorry about," she said brightly.

Too brightly, Justin thought, as she stood up and began clearing away the remains of their lunch. "Here, let me give you a hand with that," he offered.

"No need," she informed him, looking everywhere but at him. "You mentioned something earlier about taking a swim. Why don't you go ahead while I take care of this?"

Justin hesitated a moment. He could see that she was upset. What he didn't know was if she was upset because of what had almost happened between them or because he'd subjected her to the jeers of the idiots in the passing boat. Unsure what to do or say, Justin decided that maybe taking a swim wasn't such a bad idea after all.

The swim had been every bit as effective as a cold shower, Kim decided more than an hour later after she'd changed back into her shorts and top and rejoined Justin on deck. Each time she thought of how close she'd come to pleading with Justin to make love to her, she was torn between wanting to curse or thanking the boatload of revelers who'd interrupted them. There was no longer any question in her mind that Justin had wanted her. Still wanted her if she could believe that smoldering look in his eyes when she'd changed into her suit and joined him in the water.

But the scowl on his face following the other boaters' departure had confused her. So had his gruff inquiry of her. And while Justin may have kissed her like he wanted to swallow her whole a short time ago, the swim seemed to have taken the edge off his desire for her. In fact, given his relaxed appearance behind the wheel of the boat now, she could almost believe that she'd imagined those passionate kisses.

"The wind's starting to kick up a bit," Justin said. "What do you say we run up the sails and I show you what it's like to race with the wind?"

"That was absolutely incredible," Kim told him several hours later while she helped him secure the mainsail. "I felt like I was flying."

"You were," Justin informed her as he expertly knotted the ropes. "You were just doing it on top of the water."

The awkwardness following their earlier kisses had vanished sometime during those hours they'd spent zipping along the crystal-blue waters of Lake Geneva. With a patience that astonished her, Justin had kept his promise and taught her how to hoist the sails. They'd both laughed when he'd saved her from being knocked over by the boom. He'd stood beside her in the cockpit when she'd taken a turn at the wheel. And he hadn't even flinched when she'd come dangerously close to sending them onto the shore of Big Foot Beach.

"I can understand now why you love this," she told him. "What I don't know is how you could have stayed away so long."

"Right now I'm asking myself that same question," he said, his smile slipping a notch as he stared up at the sky.

She followed the direction of his gaze, noted that the sun

was already beginning to set. A wave of disappointment rolled over her as she realized the day was nearly over.

"Looks like a storm's headed this way. A big one."

Kim yanked her attention back to the weather. "That's not a problem, is it? I mean, we're already heading back to the harbor, and those dark clouds look pretty far off."

"They're just moving faster than I'd like. Can you take the wheel a minute? I'm going to drop the jib, then motor us in. The last thing I want is for your first sailing experience to end with you caught in a storm."

Kim took the wheel and kept *Calypso* steady while Justin dispatched the jib. But even with the sails down, the increased wind whistled loudly across the deck.

Justin joined her in the cockpit and started up the engine. And when Kim would have moved away to give him more room, he put his arm around her shoulders and kept her close. "What do you say we try to outrun that storm?"

Kim glanced back at the swiftly darkening sky and noted that the ugly black clouds were now much closer than they had been a few minutes ago. "You think we can beat it?"

"There's only one way to find out." He opened the engine's throttle, and *Calypso* shot forward, sending them racing toward the harbor with the wind and thunder at their backs.

Fifteen minutes later when Justin guided *Calypso* into the boat slip, fat raindrops had begun to fall. Darkness had come quickly, and the harbor, abuzz with activity and people when they'd arrived earlier that morning, now resembled a deserted graveyard of boats.

After securing the boat's lines and double-checking the cleats, Justin helped Kim from the boat. "Here, I'll take that," he told her and took her tote bag, along with the picnic basket. "Ready to make a run for the Jeep?"

"Ready," she called out to make herself heard above the shriek of the wind.

"Okay, let's go," he said. Holding hands they ran from the dock to the parking lot where Justin's Jeep now sat alone.

By the time they reached the Jeep, Kim was soaked to the skin. So was Justin. "You all right?" he asked as he started up the vehicle.

"A little wet," she said, and laughed at the understatement.

"I don't suppose you're interested in a slightly wet towel, are you?" he asked, referring to the fact that he had dropped her tote bag in a puddle while crossing the parking lot.

"Thanks. But I think I'll pass."

"We've got an hour-and-a-half drive back to Chicago. Do you want me to stop by my place at the lake and see about getting you some dry clothes? My sisters are always leaving things at my place or the main cottage. I'm sure Tara or Alexandra wouldn't mind if you borrowed something of theirs."

Kim was tempted. Not because she minded the wet clothes, but because she hated to see this day end. Still, even though earlier on the boat Justin had kissed her like a man possessed and had watched her hungrily throughout the rest of the day, he'd made no move to kiss her again. "That's okay. I'm sure I'll dry out in no time."

"All right," he said, and Kim allowed herself to believe that the disappointment she heard in his voice was because he didn't want the day to end, either.

Lost in thought, Kim didn't realize that something was wrong for several minutes, until Justin pulled the car off the road. "I need to check the wipers," he told her, and stepped out into the now driving rain.

Kim watched him through the windshield as he lifted, fiddled with and reset the wiper blades. When he got back inside the car, his face was pulled into a frown, and rain streamed down his hair and neck. "What's wrong?"

"The windshield wipers are shot." As if to show her, he flipped on the switch, and Kim noted the sluggish movement of the blade on the driver's side of the car while the blade on the passenger's side sat unmoving in the middle of the windshield. He looked at her then, his expression solemn. "I can't drive in this downpour with the wipers like this. It wouldn't be safe."

"No, it wouldn't." She bit her lower lip. "What are we going to do?"

"We can sit out the storm here in the Jeep until the worst of it is over, then I can try to find a service station and see if they can fix it."

"Is that what you think we should do?" Kim asked, and then nearly jumped out of her skin as a bolt of lightning flashed, illuminating the interior of the car. Thunder crashed a second later, causing her to jump again.

Justin said nothing for a moment, simply stared out into the night before shifting his gaze to her. His eyes met hers, held. "No. I think it would be dangerous to stay here."

"Then what do you recommend?"

"That we go to my place on the lake and wait out the storm."

Kim's heart raced as she looked into his eyes. The sexual tension that had been like a living thing between them all day seemed to snap and sizzle as he watched her and waited. "Then let's go to your place."

Justin's place was only a few minutes away. A small cottage, it was located on the large stretch of Connelly land that boasted a horse stable, several apartments and the family's lake cottage, an architectural gem designed by Frank Lloyd Wright. Kim had seen pictures of the Connellys' lake cottage featured in several architectural journals. Even in the rain the cottage looked wonderful. So did Justin's smaller version, she thought as he pulled up in front of the place and shut off the engine.

They dashed from the Jeep to the front door of the cottage, which Justin unlocked before ushering her inside.

"Damn," he muttered as he flipped the light switches and the room remained in darkness. He went to the window and looked out across the neighboring grounds that showed no signs of life or light. "It looks like the storm took out a power line." He came back to where she stood just inside the front door and looked down at her. "Will you be okay while I go see about lighting some candles?"

"I'll be fine," she told him.

"Good. Don't move. I'll be right back."

She didn't move. Instead she stood at the windows and took advantage of the floor-to-ceiling glass to watch the fireworks display being conducted by the lightning storm over the lake. Rain battered against the windowpanes, and Kim pressed her fingers against the glass. There was a savage beauty to the storm, she thought, transfixed by the power of the jagged bolts of light that sliced through the dark sky like a sword. There was something elemental and inevitable about the storm that struck some chord inside her.

"You're shivering," Justin said from behind her.

As she turned to face him, only then did Kim realize that she was indeed shivering. He draped a towel around her, pulled the ends together under her chin. "Better?" he asked.

She looked up into his hazel eyes. "Yes," she murmured. But her shaking off the chill had less to do with the dry towel and more to do with the way Justin was looking at her.

"Kim, don't look at me like that."

"Like what?"

"Like you want me."

"And if I told you that I do?" she asked, surprising herself as much as him by her boldness.

This time it was Justin who shivered. He squeezed his eyes shut, and for a moment she feared he was going to reject her. But when he opened his eyes again, the desire she saw reflected in them stole her breath. Gripping the edges of the towel, he brought her closer until her mouth was only a breath from his own.

Impatient, afraid he might change his mind yet again, Kim lifted up onto her toes and pressed her lips against his. The touch of her mouth seemed to unleash something inside him, because suddenly Justin was kissing her. Deeply. Passionately. Hungrily. When he tore his mouth free, his eyes were wild, almost savage. He didn't speak. He simply picked her up and began to carry her deeper into the house.

Thunder sounded outside, echoing the wild pounding of her heart as Justin brought her into the great room. She was vaguely aware of candles flickering about the room—on a table in front of a couch, atop the fireplace mantel, on a countertop. Flames glinted off glass vases and picture frames scattered about the room, reflected off the polished wooden floor. More flames licked from inside the fireplace where a row of candles in various shapes and sizes burned and gave the illusion of firelight.

Justin lowered her to the rug in front of the fireplace, then he knelt beside her. He removed the towel from around her shoulders and smoothed her hair. "You have the most beautiful hair," he told her as he combed his fingers into her damp tresses. "Ever since last night— No, ever since that night at the office when I saw you stretching, I've been dreaming of doing this.''

"But that night at the office, and today on the boat after we'd kissed...I thought you were angry.''

"I was angry," he explained. "With myself.''

"I don't understand.''

"I was angry because I wanted you, Kim. That night. Last night. Today. Now.''

Pleasure shot through her at his admission. "And is wanting me so wrong?''

"Maybe not wrong, but I didn't think it was fair to you. We work together. I'm your boss. You're my assistant.''

"I'm also a woman," she reminded him.

He grinned at that. "I'm well aware of that fact. I have been for some time. The number of cold showers I've taken lately are certainly proof of that. Not that it seems to have done me much good," he said as he sieved his fingers through her hair. "Because I still want you.''

Emboldened by his confession, Kim asked, "Does that mean you're going to take another cold shower?''

"Hardly. I doubt it would do any good.''

"I'm glad," she whispered. She touched his jaw, aware of the coarse stubble against her palm. She met his eyes. "Because I want you to make love to me, Justin. I have for a long time.'' Because I've loved you for a long time, she added in silence, as she slid her arms around his neck and kissed him.

She kissed him as deeply as he had kissed her. This time she pierced the seam of his lips and mated her tongue with his, trying to tell him with her mouth of the love she'd held in her heart for him all these months. She pulled at his shirt, eager to feel his skin. Justin ripped the shirt over his head and tossed it aside. Then she was kissing his neck, his mouth, tracing his nipple with her tongue while her hands roamed his chest, his back, memorized the feel of him.

"Kim," he gasped as he caught her questing fingers.

Still dazed and driven by this burning inside her for more of him, she needed a minute to focus. When she did, her courage faltered at his fierce expression. "Did I do something wrong?"

Justin groaned, squeezed his eyes shut a moment and dragged in a breath. "Sweetheart, the only one who's done anything wrong is me. I'm about to go up in flames and we've hardly started."

She eyed him warily, not sure how to respond.

His expression softened. "We're going to make love, Kim. Make no mistake about that. I'm just slowing things down a bit and giving you a chance to catch up with me."

And before she could tell him that she didn't need to catch up, that she already wanted him, he began to kiss her again. Slowly. Tenderly. Lovingly. He kissed her eyes, her mouth, her jaw. He kissed a spot just below her ear that made her shiver. Then, taking his time, he went on to her throat and planted kisses on the slope of her shoulder where her T-shirt started.

The blood sluiced through her veins, heated with each kiss until she was churning inside again and feeling as restless as the storm outside. She sought his mouth, tried to convey to him with her kiss that she didn't want to go slow. When he pulled his mouth free, Kim tried to take satisfaction in the fact that his breathing was far from steady.

He reached for the hem of her T-shirt, removed it. Excited and anxious, she was suddenly grateful for the storm and the shadowed light. As though sensing her nervousness, Justin resumed the slow kisses, pressing his moist, hot mouth to her collarbone, to the swells of her breasts. He released the catch at the front of her bra, peeled away the silky fabric, exposing her. His eyes darkened, and Kim trembled beneath the heat of his gaze, felt it like a caress.

''So beautiful. So perfect,'' he whispered as he filled his palms with her breasts.

Kim gasped as he stroked her nipples with his thumbs. Instinctively she arched her back. In answer, Justin lowered his head, laving first one nipple, then the next. When his teeth grazed the sensitive tip, Kim cried out, ''Justin!''

''It's all right. Let me love you,'' he soothed, and gentled her with another kiss as he eased her down to the pillows scattered on the rug.

Kim was sure she was on fire when Justin resumed trailing kisses down her stomach, to the waistband of her shorts. With a familiarity that would have disturbed her had she not been so awash in sensations, he removed her shorts and stripped away her panties. Then his mouth was on her again, his tongue tracing her navel, his teeth nipping her hip, the inside of her thigh.

When his fingers brushed the mouth of her sex, Kim writhed in embarrassment as she felt herself grow even more damp. ''Justin, I—''

He opened her then, began to stroke the sensitive flesh at her center with his finger. Kim could no longer think, let alone speak. Curling her fists into the towel that had fallen discarded on the rug beneath her, she could scarcely breathe as need began to spiral through her. And when Justin replaced his fingers with his mouth and stroked her with his tongue, everything inside her shattered.

Seven

Justin nearly lost it as Kim came apart beneath him, her body trembling in the throes of her climax. She was so sweet and responsive it had made holding back his own pleasure even more difficult. Witnessing her stunned look of satisfaction now as she opened her eyes and attempted to focus made him all the more glad that he had held back.

"Justin, I…you…"

He smiled, enchanted by her expressive face. He didn't need her to tell him that she was a stranger to oral sex. And he couldn't help feeling glad that he was the one to initiate her. While he knew it wasn't fair, the idea of another man touching Kim, sharing intimacies with her, struck some primal chord within him.

She touched his face. "What just happened…it was… incredible."

He kissed the palm at his jaw. "*You* were incredible," he told her, and meant it.

She smiled at him then, that woman's smile. Much like the smile he imagined the nymph Calypso had used on Odysseus. And like Odysseus, he found her impossible to resist.

She kissed him deeply, hungrily. Sitting up, she kissed his shoulder, nipped the skin, then laved it with her tongue. All the while her hands were on him, stroking, exploring. He filled his palms with her breasts, felt his manhood throb as the nipples hardened beneath his touch.

Her tongue circled his nipples, and Justin groaned when she closed her teeth around them and suckled. ''Kim, you're driving me crazy.''

''Good,'' she replied, and began a trail of kisses down his chest to his belly. After unbuckling his belt, she loosened the snap of his cutoffs. But when she fumbled with the zipper, the innocent brush of her fingers nearly sent him over the edge. Quickly, Justin dispensed with the cutoffs and briefs and returned to Kim.

''You're beautiful,'' she whispered, and ran her fingers down his male length.

The sensation was erotic and as arousing as hell. Like being stroked by velvet, Justin thought. When she closed her fist around him, his vision blurred. ''Kim, sweetheart,'' he cautioned, and captured her wrist. Sucking in a breath, he grappled for control. He'd been teetering on the edge since she'd kissed him and told him she wanted him. He didn't want to ruin it for both of them by exploding now.

Trying to slow things down again, he pressed her back into the pillows and kissed her softly.

It didn't work. How could it? he reasoned when she was nipping his mouth with her teeth? When she was guiding him to her moist center? When she was looking up at him out of those incredible blue-green eyes that mirrored his own desire? With a Herculean effort, Justin held himself back and forced himself to ask, ''Are you sure this is what you want? It'll probably kill me to stop now, but I will if you're not sure.''

''I'm sure,'' she told him, and pulled his mouth down to hers. ''I want this. I want *you*.''

The kiss was hot, explosive, carnal. Justin wasn't sure where his mouth ended and where Kim's began. He only knew that he couldn't get close enough to her. She moved against him, brushing her lower body against his sex. He went weak with need as she guided him to her warm, moist center.

''Wait,'' he told her, feeling the last vestiges of his sanity and control slip. He scanned the shadows, searching the floor for his pants, intent on getting protection.

''Please, Justin. Now!''

And before he could stop her, Kim was lifting her hips.

Justin swore. Unable to stop himself, he caught her hips and drove himself home. He felt the brief resistance, heard Kim's soft cry and froze as he realized the reason behind it. He tried to remain perfectly still, terrified that he would hurt her even more.

''Justin?''

''Sweetheart, try not to move,'' he told her when she stirred beneath him. Sweat broke out across his brow with the effort it took him not to finish what they'd begun. ''I don't want to hurt you any more than I already have.''

She caught his face between her palms and forced him to look at her. ''You didn't hurt me. But you will if you tell me that my being a virgin makes a difference and you no longer want me.''

''Oh, I want you.'' He wanted her as he'd never wanted anyone or anything before in his life.

''Then show me.''

''Kim—''

She tightened her feminine muscles, and Justin groaned at the sensation.

Lightning flashed outside, illuminating the room with streaks of light. Thunder struck nearby. But the storm outside was no match for the storm inside him as Kim began to move beneath him. Then all he could see was Kim. All he wanted was Kim.

Driven by desire and the need to make this special for her, to make her his, Justin eased his hand between them and began to stroke that sensitive spot with his finger even as he moved himself inside her. He brought her up, took her to the brink.

Her eyes were glazed as she looked at him and gasped, "Justin, I can't. I—"

"You can," he assured her, urging her to take. When she shuddered, cried out in wonder, Justin's own need spiked. Drinking in her cries of pleasure, he strained to hold himself back as she pulsed around him and brought him closer and closer to the edge.

Sweat trickled down his back with the effort it took not to follow her over the crest into those storm-tossed waves. Still, he waited. And when her spasms subsided, he took her up again and again, and watched her come apart in his arms. While he liked to believe he was a generous lover, never before had he felt this need to give so much. Never before had he found such pleasure in the giving.

When she pulsed around him and cried out his name, his control broke. He plunged into her one last time and the world around him exploded as he followed Kim into the storm.

Now he knew what it must feel like to be shipwrecked, Justin thought a short time later. He eased himself up onto his elbows and looked down at Kim. Something warm and tender unfurled inside him as he stared at her flushed face. He pressed a kiss to her mouth. "Are you all right?"

Her lashes fluttered, and she opened her eyes. A smile curved her lips. "Am I alive?"

"I think so," he told her, feeling a measure of relief at her response. "You're sure I didn't hurt you?"

"Positive. You're a wonderful lover, Justin Connelly. Just as I knew you would be."

Justin sobered at the reminder of the gift she'd given him. He lay down beside her and held her in the circle of his arms. Kissing the top of her head, he asked, "Will you be all right by yourself for a few minutes? There's something I want to do."

"Yes, but—"

He silenced her with a kiss. "No buts. Wait here. I'll be right back."

Snagging his cutoffs, Justin took one of the candles from the mantel and headed for the bathroom, where he turned on the taps and began to fill the old-fashioned claw-foot tub with water. Once he had the tub filled and had lit the room with the fat, scented candles Tara had insisted he needed the last time she visited, he went to retrieve Kim.

She lay sleeping on the rug in front of the fireplace where he'd left her. With the towel wrapped around her body, her arms and legs were bare. For several moments Justin stood over her and watched the candlelight play over her features. She looked so beautiful and tempting that he wondered how on earth he had managed to work with her for six months and not realize it.

But on some level he had recognized just how beautiful and special Kim was, Justin admitted as he knelt beside her and brushed a strand of hair from her face. He'd simply tried his best to ignore it and his feelings for Kim because deep down inside he'd known that once he did acknowledge them, he and Kim would find themselves right where they were now. As lovers.

When it came to making decisions, he and Kim becoming lovers was probably not the wisest thing to do, Justin conceded. After all, he'd seen firsthand just how his father's involvement with his former secretary Angie Donahue had impacted his parents' marriage. Though his parents had patched up their differences and his mother had raised his half brother, Seth, as her own, it had not been easy for any of them, including Seth. That was why Justin had been determined to avoid just such a situation by ignoring his attraction to Kim.

But then, he and Kim were not his father and Seth's mother, he reasoned. And he was no longer sure he'd really had any choice in the matter. Even now, less than thirty minutes since he'd made love to her, he wanted her again with an intensity that shook him.

Kim stirred, and when she opened her eyes, she asked, "Where did you go?"

"I'll show you," he said, and slid his arms beneath her legs and lifted her. He carried her into the bathroom, where he removed the towel she'd draped over her body and lowered her into the tub. Reaching for the hair clip he'd found stashed in a drawer, he gathered her hair onto her head to keep it from getting wet again.

"Thank you," she murmured, and eased down into the tub of bubbles.

Justin picked up the sponge, dipped it in the water, then began moving it gently along her leg, up the inside of her thigh.

Kim stilled his hand. "You don't have to do that."

"I know I don't have to. I want to." When her fingers remained locked around his wrist, he met her gaze and explained, "You gave me the most incredible gift a little while ago, Kim. Had I known, I would have tried to be more gentle.''

''You were gentle. I told you, you were wonderful.''

''Not gentle enough. I wanted you too badly.''

''But—''

''Please,'' he said. ''Let me do this. Let me show you gentleness now.''

He showed her.

Though he never planned for the gentle bathing of her tender flesh as foreplay, there was no denying that he was fully aroused when he lifted her from the tub and wrapped her in the bath sheet. He just hoped that Kim wouldn't notice.

She noticed.

At least, Justin assumed she'd noticed because he caught the hint of a smile on her lips when she reached for the body lotion and brushed her hip up against his zipper. He bit off a groan.

''Sorry,'' she said, but the contrite tone didn't match her expression.

He wanted her. And watching her smooth lotion on her legs wasn't helping. Despite the bath, he knew darned well that she had to be tender from their earlier lovemaking. Only a beast would consider making love to her again now.

''You mentioned something about a bathrobe earlier?''

Justin jerked his gaze from her legs to her face. ''Yeah. I think Tara left one in the bedroom closet. I'll go get it for you.''

He returned in time to see her release her hair from the clip and send long, blond waves cascading down her bare shoulders and back. Justin swallowed hard. Deciding the only way he was going to be able to keep his hands off her was to make himself scarce, he said, ''Here you go. I don't know about you, but I'm starved. I'm going to go raid the kitchen and see if I can find us something to eat.''

While he was at it, he was going to stand outside and pray that the rain cooled him off.

The rain didn't cool him off. Nor did sharing the remainder of the pâté and French bread from their lunch and washing it down with one of the bottles of wine he'd found in the liquor cabinet. Somehow the simple meal became a sensual minefield. And before he knew it, they were kissing again. One kiss strung into another and another, until he ended up carrying Kim and the opened bottle of wine upstairs to the bedroom.

He made love to her again. This time he loved her slowly. Gently. Completely. And when he lowered her onto his shaft and joined their bodies, she rode him. He filled his palms with her breasts, gloried in the sight of her astride him as she set the pace. She moved slowly, sensuously, her face reflecting her shock and pleasure as sensation rolled through her. When she increased the tempo, Justin clutched her hips and matched her pace. And when she cried out his name, Justin flipped her beneath him and raced to join her as she plunged into the storm.

Kim blinked at the wash of bright sunshine streaming through the window. She glanced around the unfamiliar room and bed, noted the man's arm draped over her, the hand closed possessively over her breast. Then she remembered. Justin. The sailboat. The storm. Memories of the night came rushing back to her. Of Justin telling her he wanted her. Of his hands and mouth on her. Of her own hands and mouth on him. Heat flooded her cheeks as she recalled the intimacies she'd shared with him, of how completely she'd surrendered her body and heart to him.

Making love with Justin had been the most beautiful experience of her life. If this was how her mother had felt, she could understand now why Amanda Lindgren had spent her life searching to find love like this a second time when her relationship with Kim's father hadn't worked out. Kim thought of how loving Justin had been with her. How he had bathed her so gently, the tender way he had looked at her as he'd brought her to his bed. His every touch, his every look had been filled with love. Only, he'd never given her the words, she reminded herself.

Kim bit her lip, remembered how difficult it had been for her to keep the words locked inside. Yet even in those intense moments when Justin had filled her, merged their bodies as one, he'd cried out how much he wanted her, needed her. But never once had he said that he loved her.

And he hadn't said that he loved her because he didn't love her, Kim reasoned.

You knew that going in, Kim. Did you really think that because you slept together Justin would fall in love with you?

Kim frowned at the nagging voice in her head, knew it was true. She was neither naive nor foolish enough to delude herself into believing that last night meant as much to Justin as it had to her. Why should it? He'd been a perfect gentleman, had given her more than one chance to call a halt before things had gone too far. But she hadn't ended it, because she had wanted Justin to make love to her, had practically begged him to do so, she admitted. And if she was going to be honest, she might as well admit that the moment she realized Justin actually desired her, nothing short of death would have made her say no last night.

The problem was, what did she do now? How did one act the morning after spending the night in the boss's bed? Kim fisted her fingers in the sheets and wished she hadn't shied away from those Monday-morning coffee-and-sex chats that went on among a few of her female co-workers. If she had listened, she might have a clue as to just what she was supposed to do this morning. Did she say thank you and tell him what a fantastic lover he was? Or was it considered more savvy to act as though nothing extraordinary had happened? And what about when she went back to work on Monday? Kim bit back a moan as she considered the awkwardness of sitting across a desk from Justin and remembering that he had seen her naked. That she had seen him naked. If only—

"Do you always wake up so tense?"

Kim's heart leaped at the sound of Justin's voice. Unsure what to do, what to say, she simply froze.

Justin reached for her sheet-tangled fingers, and her breath hitched as his arm grazed her breasts. After tugging the fabric free, he coaxed her to turn over so that she faced him. He'd pushed up onto his elbow and was staring down into her face, and all she could think was how handsome he looked, with his hair mussed, whiskers shadowing his jaw and his mouth curved into a wicked grin.

"Good morning," he told her, and brushed his mouth against hers.

"Morning." Kim finally managed to get the words past her lips.

He frowned. "You okay?"

"I'm fine," she lied. She was nervous, confused, unsure.

He eyed her closely. "Any regrets about last night?"

"No," she answered honestly. She didn't regret making love with him. How could she regret something so beautiful? So right? But it was obvious from his somber expression that Justin did have regrets. "What about you? Do you regret what happened?"

The smile he gave her was fleeting. "Not making love to you. What you gave me...it was a wonderful and special gift, Kim. But what I do regret was not being more gentle that first time. I'm sorry I hurt you.''

''I told you, you didn't hurt me.'' When he arched his brow in disbelief, she conceded, ''Well, it only hurt a little and just for a moment.''

''Thank you for that,'' he said softly.

''It's the truth,'' she told him, and tried to decipher the reason for the worry line that creased his brow. She'd worked too closely with him during the past six months not to recognize that something was bothering him. ''Are you sure you don't regret what happened between us, Justin?''

His expression softened, and he stroked her cheek with the same tenderness he had exhibited when he'd bathed her last night. ''I'm sure. I'm just wishing I hadn't been so out of my head with desire for you that I didn't use any protection the first time we made love.''

''Oh.''

'''Oh' is right,'' Justin responded. ''Even if you're on birth control pills, using protection would have been the smart thing to do.''

Especially since she wasn't on the pill, Kim added in silence. Suddenly the repercussions of last night hit her like a dash of cold water in the face. The room spun. Justin's voice echoed through her head. All she could think of was her mother. How Amanda Lindgren had ended up pregnant and alone because her lover hadn't loved her. How the man who had fathered her hadn't even been free to love her mother because he was already married. An image of herself alone and pregnant flitted through Kim's mind. She sat up, hugged the sheet around her breasts.

''Kim?'' Justin cupped her shoulders and gave her a tiny shake. ''Kim, sweetheart, what is it?''

She met his eyes, registered his concern. ''I'm not on the pill.''

Justin's gaze shifted from her face to her abdomen, then back to her eyes. "You...if we..." he whooshed out a breath. "If there's a baby because of last night, you have my word that I'll take full responsibility for you and our child."

It had never occurred to her that Justin would be anything less than honorable. But as much as she loved him, the last thing she wanted was a relationship with him based on obligation. Feeling far too vulnerable with only the sheet as protection, Kim reached for the robe lying on the floor beside the bed. She slipped it on and walked over to the window and stared out at the blue sky.

"Kim?" Justin said from behind her. He turned her around to face him. "I meant what I said. I'll take care of you and the baby if there is one. So please don't worry that you'll be alone, because you won't."

"I know that. And I'm not worried. Really I'm not. Last night...well, it was a safe time for me. The chances of my getting pregnant...well, they're slim." She fibbed and prayed it was the truth.

"Slim or not, it's still a possibility," Justin reminded her. "In the future I promise to be more responsible about using protection."

Talk of pregnancy and the future stripped away any illusions she'd harbored, and sobered Kim as nothing else could. She knew in that moment that she could never settle for an affair with Justin, and an affair was all that he was offering. "Actually, I'm not sure continuing this is a good idea."

Justin dropped his hands from her shoulders. "What are you saying? You said you didn't regret last night."

"I don't. Last night was wonderful. But it wasn't smart for either of us. I think the wise thing to do is forget last night ever happened."

Justin's eyes hardened. "I'm afraid that isn't going to be possible. You see, I made love with *you* last night—not just a warm body. And contrary to what you obviously believe, I don't just hop into bed with a woman and forget about it. Considering the fact that you were a virgin until last night, I know damn well it's not something you do on a regular basis, either. So don't insult both of us by insinuating that last night didn't mean anything. Because it did."

"Of course it meant something to me," she retorted. Moving past him, she pressed her lips together tightly and blinked hard to keep back the tears burning behind her eyes. When she had regained control of herself, she turned to face him. "I care about you, Justin. And it's obvious that I'm attracted to you. That we're attracted to each other."

"So what's the problem?"

"The problem is that sooner or later an affair has to end. And when it does, things can get messy." She held up her hand when he started to speak. "I love my job. I love working with you. Having an affair would jeopardize that."

"How?" Justin asked.

"Because when the affair's over, it would be impossible for us to go on working together."

"Who says it has to end?" he argued.

"It would."

He moved closer, tucked a strand of hair behind her ear. "I care about you, Kim."

Kim's heart ached because she knew what he said was true. He did care about her. He just didn't love her. And it was his love that she wanted. "Then don't ask me to risk losing what I value most—your friendship and my job. Because that's what I'd be doing. Can't we just go back to the way things were before last night?"

"Is that really what you want? To forget last night ever happened?"

''That's what I want,'' she said, even though she knew she would never be able to forget last night or how much it had meant to her.

''All right,'' Justin said, and there was such desolation in his voice, in his eyes, that for a moment Kim thought she might actually have hurt him. ''I'll try to do what you've asked.''

''Thank you.''

''Don't thank me yet. I said I'd try. That doesn't mean I'll succeed.''

''I understand,'' Kim replied.

''Then you should also understand that if you're pregnant, all bets are off. And there's no way you'll be able to keep me out of your life or our baby's life.''

Everything Kim had said made sense, Justin reminded himself as he sat at the dinner table at his parents' Lake Shore home more than a week later. The fact that he and Kim worked together made a romantic involvement between them potentially messy. One of the larger textile importers in the country, Connelly Corporation was like a small city unto itself—which meant people talked—and among their favorite topics was the Connelly family members and their personal lives. So a personal relationship with him would only subject Kim to gossip. He didn't want that.

No, a boss-employee relationship simply wasn't smart, Justin told himself again. For proof of that fact he had only to look to his brother Seth and the slights he had suffered because his mother had been Grant Connelly's secretary. Kim had been right to call a halt to things between them. She'd been right to insist they forget about that night at the cottage and what had happened between them. That was why he had respected her wishes, done what she'd asked and firmly closed that door.

And it wasn't working worth spit.

Disgusted, Justin closed his fist around the stem of his wineglass and admitted the truth. He hadn't been able to forget a minute of that day and night he'd spent with Kim. He couldn't look at her without remembering how beautiful she'd looked by firelight with her hair flowing down about her shoulders like silk, with her head tipped back and her cheeks flushed, with that look of utter wonder on her face as she'd ridden him. Nor could he forget how soft her skin had felt, how she had trembled when he'd touched her, how perfectly her body had fitted with his. And if he lived to be a hundred, he didn't think he would ever be able to forget how sweet her lips had tasted or the way he had felt when she'd climaxed and cried out his name.

Dammit! Justin slammed down his glass on the table. This business of pretending nothing had happened between him and Kim wasn't working.

"Is there a problem with your wine, Justin?"

Justin yanked his gaze to the end of the table at the sound of his father's voice, and only then realized that everyone at the table had gone silent. All eyes were fixed on the glass he held in a death grip. A quick scan revealed he had come dangerously close to spilling wine on his mother's lace tablecloth. "No, sir. The wine is fine," he told his father and to prove it, he took a sip of the merlot. "I'm sorry. My mind was somewhere else."

His father frowned, deepening the creases in his tanned face. "You've seemed distracted quite a lot lately. Is there a problem at the office?"

"Nothing I can't handle, sir."

When his father started to pursue that line of questioning, Emma Connelly placed her hand on her husband's arm.

"Leave the boy alone, Grant. If Justin said it's nothing to worry about, then there's nothing to worry about. We have more pressing problems than Connelly Corporation."

Justin knew at once that his mother was referring to the assassination attempt on his brother Daniel several months ago. Noting the worried expression on his mother's face, Justin felt a rush of guilt that he'd been so wrapped up over his own dilemma concerning Kim that he'd barely given his older brother's situation a thought. So he paid attention now when his mother focused her sad blue eyes on his brother Brett's wife, Elena, who had been the police detective called in to investigate the attempt on Daniel's life.

"Elena, dear, I know this isn't the appropriate time or place, and it probably goes against your regulations as a police detective, but can you tell me if you've been able to turn up anything new in your investigation?"

"I'm afraid not. While we're sure whoever tried to kill Daniel was a pro, so far we haven't been able to come up with any solid leads on who contracted the hit. I'm sorry. I wish I had better news."

Grant tossed down his napkin and leaned forward, a forbidding expression on his face. Despite his sixty-five years, there was no mistaking the determination and presence of power he wore like a mantle. His father still possessed the same air of invincibility that had enabled him to found the Connelly dynasty, Justin thought. "This is taking too long. I want the person or persons responsible for trying to kill my son found," Grant informed his daughter-in-law.

"That's what we all want," Elena told him, and Justin gave her credit for not flinching under Grant's granite gaze. "This case has been given top priority, Grant. We're doing everything we can to find them."

"We know you are, dear," Emma said, taking some of the sting out of her husband's words. "Don't we, Grant?"

His father covered Emma's hand that lay on his sleeve. When he looked up again, his steel-gray eyes had softened. "Yes, we know you're doing everything possible, Elena. I'm sorry if I sounded like I believed otherwise. I just don't like knowing that there's someone out there who's willing to go to such lengths to eliminate one of my children."

"I understand," Elena told him.

"Find out who's responsible and stop them, Elena. Please."

"We will," Elena promised. She slanted a glance to her husband, Brett, who sat beside her, and Justin tried to decipher the look that passed between them. "I was going to wait until tomorrow to tell you this in my official capacity, but I don't see any point in waiting now. Because of my pregnancy and the direction this case is taking, I've decided to turn the investigation over to a colleague of mine named Tom Reynolds and his partner Lucas Starwind."

"Is there anything wrong with the baby?" Emma asked.

"No. But Brett and I don't want to take any chances," Elena explained, and Justin recalled his brother telling him that prior to this pregnancy, Elena had suffered two miscarriages.

"These detectives—Reynolds and Starwind—are they as good as you?" Grant asked.

"Tom's first-rate. He's the one who showed me the ropes when I joined the police force. I'd trust him with my life."

"And Starwind?" Grant prompted.

"Him I don't know much about. But he's Tom's partner, and according to Tom he's good. Real good. And that's a direct quote from Tom, who's known for being flat-out stingy when it comes to handing out praise," Elena explained. "I have every confidence that between the two of them, they'll find out who's behind the attempt on Daniel's life."

"Then we'll trust them to put an end to this nightmare, too," Emma declared. "The important thing for you is to take care of yourself and our future grandchild."

"Don't worry, she will," Brett offered. "I'll see to that."

Justin stared at his younger brother and Elena, saw a look pass between them. He'd seen that same look before between his parents and grandparents—an unspoken communication that signaled they were one. Justin's gaze dropped, and he noted the way Elena's and Brett's joined hands rested on her swollen stomach.

Once more Justin's thoughts turned to Kim, and he recalled his shock upon realizing they had used no form of protection that first time they'd made love. Despite Kim's claims, there was a possibility she could be pregnant with his child.

And if she was?

The idea didn't shake him nearly as much now as it had earlier. All right, he told himself. He'd tried things Kim's way, and it wasn't working, for either of them, if those dark circles he'd seen under Kim's eyes meant anything. So maybe it was time to try things his way.

Eight

"**W**orking late again, Kim?" Dina Dietrich asked as she stood at the elevator with several other members of the clerical staff who were leaving for the day.

"Just for a few minutes," Kim replied, and silently cursed her luck. Another five minutes and she would have missed Dina. While she got along well with most of her co-workers, there were a few females who were much too catty for her taste. And Dina Dietrich was the worst. Ever since she had lost out to Kim on the position as Justin's assistant, she never missed the chance to make some snide remark or try to embarrass her in front of the other employees. "As soon as I finish up these memos for Mr. Connelly, I'll be on my way."

"Oh, I didn't realize that Justin still expected you to call him Mr. Connelly," Dina said, the sly look in her eyes belying her innocent tone.

Kim bit back her temper at the innuendo—one of several

she'd endured since Robert Marsh had "accidentally" mentioned that she had gone sailing with Justin. From what her friends had told her, Marsh's spin on the bachelor auction was that Kim had emptied her savings account to make the winning bid. According to Marsh, the reason Kim seldom dated was because she'd set her sights on marrying rich. And who fit that bill better than a Connelly? The sailing date was supposedly the first step in her grand scheme to land Justin. Despite Marsh's denials when she'd confronted him, Kim didn't doubt for a minute that he was behind the gossip. The tale had made her the center of office scuttlebutt for more than two weeks. And a prime target for Dina. Determined not to take the bait, Kim kept her voice level and said, "No, he doesn't expect me to call him Mr. Connelly. I do so out of respect since he's my boss."

Obviously aware that she was playing to an audience, Dina made a show of scanning the area for eavesdroppers before lowering her voice conspiratorially and asking, "Come on, Kim. You don't really expect me to believe that you spent the weekend with the man and didn't even call him by his first name, do you?"

"The truth is, Dina, I don't really care what you believe," Kim said, gripping the files she held tightly to stop her hands from trembling with anger. She met the sultry brunette's green eyes. "But if I were you, I'd think twice before spreading gossip about Justin Connelly. While you may find it amusing to make insinuations about my reputation and character, I doubt that the Connellys would find it amusing if they were to discover you've been making disparaging innuendos about one of its family members. Someone who not only happens to be a vice president of this company, but who also happens to be your boss."

For once Dina remained speechless. And had the floor

not been carpeted, Kim was sure she would have been able to hear a pin drop. The ding of the elevator, announcing its arrival, echoed loudly in the silence. Choosing that moment to make her exit, Kim said, "Have a good evening." Without waiting for a response, she turned and headed for her office.

Once she was alone, all the fury she'd held in check came rushing to the surface. Kim slapped the folders she'd been holding on top of her desk. It was all Robert Marsh's fault, she fumed. She curled her hands into fists at her sides. For two cents she would gladly wring the man's neck. Feeling as though she was about to explode, she closed her eyes and silently counted to ten in an effort to calm down.

When counting to ten didn't work, she started over and went to twenty. Twice. Seventeen. Eighteen. Nineteen. She ran through the numbers again in her head, but to no avail. It wasn't helping. Frustrated and still angry enough to chew nails, she kicked her chair, pretending it was Robert Marsh's head.

Kim yelped as pain radiated up her leg, and she grabbed her foot.

"You have a disagreement with the chair?"

Kim nearly groaned at the sound of Justin's voice behind her. Feeling like an idiot, she released her aching foot, and turned to face him. "My foot slipped," she offered, unable to come up with any reasonable excuse for pounding on the company's furniture.

While he didn't call her on the fib, he slanted a glance downward to where she was rubbing her aching toe against the back of her calf. "You probably bruised your toe. Why don't I have a look and—"

"No," Kim fired back, and retreated a step. Swallowing past the panic, she said more calmly, "I mean, my foot's fine. Really. If you're looking for those memos on the Genome Project, I have them right here for your signature.'' Turning away from the questions in his hazel eyes, she retrieved the file folder containing the transcribed memos from her desk. Then she handed it to Justin.

He hesitated a moment. There was something sad and vulnerable in his expression before he took the folder she offered. ''Thank you,'' he said, and retreated into his office.

For several moments Kim stood there, staring after him. That couldn't have possibly been hurt in Justin's eyes when she'd shied away from him, could it? No, she told herself. More than likely it was disappointment because the great sex—or at least she thought it had been great—would not be repeated. And if she felt some disappointment of her own at the decision, she reminded herself it was best to end things now. Otherwise she stood a good chance of falling into that hopeless trap of believing that Justin might actually love her someday the way she loved him. She'd spent too many years watching her mother spin dreams of happily-ever-after only to come crashing down when they didn't happen. She wouldn't put herself through that same torture. No, it was best to deal in reality. And the reality of the situation was that she and Justin were not going to happen. Besides, she had enough on her plate now without adding impossible dreams to it.

Kim glanced at the open calendar on her desk and felt that tiny flutter of panic. She was now nearly three weeks late for her menstrual cycle—and she'd never, ever been this late before. She worried her bottom lip and recalled the fib she'd told Justin about it being a safe time for her. She prayed her words wouldn't come back to haunt her.

''Kim, I have a few more minor changes,'' Justin said as he came up behind her. ''I'd appreciate it if you'd make them before you leave.''

''Be glad to.''

"And when you're finished, I'd like to take you to dinner. If you're free this evening."

"Thanks, but I'm afraid I already have plans for this evening." So maybe doing her laundry wasn't exactly what he thought she meant, but she did have to do it.

"What about tomorrow?"

"I'm going to be busy."

"Sunday?" he countered, his mouth going flat.

"Tied up. Now if you'll excuse me, I'd better get these changes done or I'll be late."

"All right," he conceded. "But sooner or later you and I are going to talk. You can't go on avoiding me forever."

Kim did manage to avoid him—or at least avoid talking to him—for most of the next week, thanks in large measure to an unexpected emergency that had taken Justin back to New York. When he returned on Friday, he'd been in a bear of a mood and so busy she'd had little trouble avoiding any personal conversation. She watched the clock on her desk, noted the hands edging just past five o'clock. This had nothing to do with being a coward, Kim assured herself as she gathered up the mail and notes and headed for Justin's office. She would dump his messages and correspondence on his desk while he was still on the phone and get out the door before he even knew she was gone. Bracing herself, she tapped lightly on his door and prayed her luck would hold out a little longer.

She stepped inside his office, and Justin hung up the phone. Kim knew at once that her luck had run out. "I have a few messages for you, the letters you dictated and the financial reports you wanted." Quickly dispensing with the items, she said, "If there's nothing else, I'm going to call it a day."

"Actually, I'd like you to bring me up to speed on several projects. Would you mind staying a few minutes longer?"

Kim hesitated but saw no way around it. "No problem," she said, and took a seat across from him. For the next fifteen minutes Justin went over routine business matters and projects, and Kim began to relax.

"What about that problem we had a while ago with the computer system? That technician Charlotte Masters hired seems to have done a good job. Everything running okay?"

"Yes. Everything seems to be running smoothly now," Kim assured him.

Justin nodded. "Is there anything else we need to cover?"

Kim glanced at her notes, then back up at him. "No. You should be up to speed on everything in the department now."

"Good." He put down his pen, sat back in his chair and stared at her. "Now we can talk about us."

Kim's stomach fluttered. "Us?"

"Yes, Kim. Us," he said, an edge in his voice. He sat forward. "As in you and me. Or maybe you've done such a good job of pretending nothing happened between us that night in the cottage that you've forgotten we were lovers."

"Hardly," Kim shot back, not bothering to hide the irony of his claim. Since she was now nearly four weeks late, she might have an even more tangible reminder of that night.

Evidently reading something in her expression, Justin's eyes widened. "Kim, What are you saying? Are you...?" His gaze dropped to her belly, then shot back to her face. He stood, started around the desk. "No wonder you haven't been yourself. Sweetheart, you should have told me. I promised you that if you became pregnant, I'd take responsibility. And I will. All you had—"

His words swiped at Kim's heart. She rushed to her feet. "First off, there's no reason for you to panic, because I don't know whether I'm pregnant or not," Kim told him, reasoning it was true since she'd yet to take a pregnancy test. "And second, if I am pregnant, I have a generous employer who provides an excellent salary and benefits, so I'm quite capable of taking care of myself and a baby if it comes to it. And third," she ticked off her finger as temper took hold. "I'm not out to trap you into a relationship you don't want. So there's no need for you to worry on that score."

"Are you finished?" Justin asked her, his voice deadly soft, his expression inscrutable.

Refusing to be intimidated, she jutted out her chin and met his hazel eyes. "Yes."

"Then let me set you straight on a few things. First off, I never panic. Second, I know Connelly's salaries and benefits are generous, since I had a hand in drawing them up. And third," he said menacingly as he caught her by the shoulders and pulled her to within a breath of him, "I'm not the one who needs to be worried about getting trapped into a relationship I don't want. You are."

And before she could even think of a response, Justin kissed her. His mouth was hard, angry, demanding. When his tongue demanded entry, she didn't even try to resist. She opened to him. Someone moaned. Kim didn't know if it was her or Justin. All she knew was that she was drowning in sensation, in the need for more. No longer innocent, her body knew the joys of making love with this man and responded accordingly. She roped her arms around him, took and demanded, even as she gave. When she felt the weight of his arousal pressed against her belly, an answering need throbbed inside her.

He lifted his head and speared his fingers through her

hair, loosening the pins. "Kim, I—" Suddenly, Justin stilled. He dropped his hands to her shoulders.

"Justin, what is it?"

"Shh." He pressed his fingers to her lips and looked past her toward the door.

Kim turned slightly, stared in the direction that had caught his attention, and she noted that the door had been left ajar. But as far as she could tell, they were alone. She shifted her gaze to him and waited for him to explain.

"I thought I saw someone at the door," he said as he released her and walked over to the door to investigate.

Kim thought of the kiss they had just shared, and instinctively, she reached up and smoothed a hand over her hair. She nearly groaned as she imagined Dina Dietrich or one of her cohorts getting an eyeful of her kissing Justin. Considering her conversation with the other woman just a short time ago, she knew the office rumor mill would have a field day.

"I don't see anyone," Justin told her when he returned to her side. "We need to talk, Kim. But I'm supposed to be meeting Marsh in a few minutes."

The mention of Robert Marsh sobered Kim. He was the last person she wanted to have find her alone with Justin, her hair mussed and her lipstick ruined. "I'll get out of your way."

"You're not in my way, and you and I have some unfinished business to discuss," he told her, and gave her a quick, hard kiss. "Personal business," he clarified. "But I could be a while with Marsh. I'll call you later."

He didn't ask if he could call her, simply told her he intended to do so, Kim noted. But before she could call him on it, there was a tap at his door and Robert Marsh was sticking his head inside.

"Am I interrupting?" he asked, flashing them a smile

that Kim thought was as slick and phony as the man himself.

"I was just leaving," Kim replied coolly and started past Marsh toward the door. "Good night, Justin."

"Here, let me get that for you," Marsh said politely, and opened the door for her.

"Thank you," she murmured.

"My pleasure," he told her.

One look at the gleam in his eyes and Kim's stomach knotted like a fist. Marsh had seen her kissing Justin. She knew it in her heart. She could only hope that he hadn't also heard their conversation.

"Hi, this is Kim. I'm not able to come to the phone right now. Leave a message and I'll get back to you."

Justin slammed down the telephone. Shoving his hands through his hair, he paced the length of his apartment. Where in the devil could she be? he asked himself as he stared out the window and watched the sun begin its descent in the sky. He considered driving by her apartment again, but nixed the idea. He'd driven by twice yesterday and once today already. And it was the memory of his last attempt to see her that ate at him now.

He scrubbed a hand down his face as he recalled the scene a few hours ago.

He'd hit the buzzer on the door repeatedly, and when she hadn't answered, he'd rapped on the door. "Come on, Kim. Open the door." Frustrated by the game she was playing, he'd knocked again and told her, "Sweetheart, I saw your car parked outside, so I know you're in there."

"No, she's not."

Justin had spun around to see a pair of faded brown eyes in a weathered face watching him through the crack between the door and the safety chain. Despite the woman's orange-colored hair and rouged cheeks, Justin made her to be seventy if she was a day. Realizing that he was staring, he cleared his throat and said, "I was trying to reach Kim. I'm sorry if I disturbed you."

"You didn't disturb me," she said matter-of-factly. "But, like I told you, Kim's not home. She left early yesterday morning."

Uneasiness coiled in his gut at that news. Since he knew Kim had no family, he couldn't help wondering where Kim had gone that she would have left her car. And why had she gone when she'd known he'd wanted to see her? Because she wanted to get away—from him. Deciding his best hope of finding her was the little old lady sizing him up, he tried turning on the charm. "I'm Justin Connelly," he said. "Kim's my assistant."

"I'm Lucille Brown."

He flashed her a smile. "A pleasure Ms. Brown. I was wondering, do—"

"It's Miss," she informed him. After releasing the safety chain, she opened the door wider to reveal a tiny woman in a bright green running suit. She smiled at him. "I'm still waiting for Mr. Right to come along."

Justin cleared his throat. Given her age, he suspected that Mr. Right had come and gone some time ago. "Um, Miss Brown—"

"You can call me Lucy," she told him, and batted her eyelashes at him.

"Um, Lucy, would you happen to know where Kim went?"

"She said she was going to spend the weekend at the beach with her friend."

"Her friend," Justin repeated, more to himself than to Lucy, as he tried to remember if there was anyone in particular that Kim gravitated to among the office staff. "Did Kim happen to mention the name of this friend?"

"No, but it was the same young man who came by for her a couple of weeks ago."

Justin's blood iced, then ran hot in his veins.

"Whoever he is, he's a good-looking one. Almost as tall as you, with nice, tight buns."

Justin nearly choked. "Thanks, Lucy," he murmured and made his exit.

Several hours later jealousy was like a beast clawing inside him. The idea of Kim with someone else, with another man kissing her, touching her as he had, put blood in his eye. He needed to beat something or someone, Justin decided. Preferably the man who was with Kim. But since he didn't know who the guy was yet, he'd settle for picking a fight with one of his brothers. Every one of the Connellys was good with his fists. He'd never known any of them to shy from a fight, particularly if goaded properly. Since he possessed the same quick temper, it shouldn't be too difficult to get the fists flying, he reasoned. And maybe if he was busy pounding on one of his brothers and being pounded on in return, he wouldn't have time to think about Kim. And whom she was with, or what she was doing with him.

Snatching up his car keys, Justin headed for Brett's house.

"All that baiting wasted," Justin complained as a smiling Brett and Elena waved goodbye. For a moment, there, he'd been sure Brett was going to take a swing at him. Then Elena had come in, showing him some things she'd picked up for the baby, and his tough, take-no-prisoners brother had turned into a marshmallow.

"Disgusting," Justin muttered as he pointed his Jeep toward Seth's. Seth was who he should have gone to in the first place, Justin decided. Seth was always up for a fight. Probably because he was sensitive to the fact that his birth had been the result of his mother's affair with their father. While Justin might understand some of Seth's feelings of not quite belonging, he couldn't honestly identify with them. As far as Justin was concerned, Seth was a Connelly. It didn't matter who had given birth to him, Emma Connelly considered him her son—and that was good enough for Justin.

Didn't anyone stay home anymore? Justin wondered as he put the Jeep into reverse and sped away from Seth's place. He considered going to his brother Rafe's, then decided against it since he wasn't sure if Rafe was even in town. Instead he opted for the gym—where he pounded on the bag until his arms ached and fed his blood lust by sparring with an up-and-coming professional boxer.

By the time he arrived at Connelly Corporation headquarters the next morning, Justin's mood matched the dark shiner he sported on his left eye courtesy of yesterday's sparring match. And it was in keeping with his string of bad luck that the first person he saw was Brett.

Brett whistled. "That's a real beauty you've got there. The shade almost matches your suit."

"You're a real comedian," Justin told him with a scowl, and continued on to his office. He'd slept little the previous night, imagining Kim with some unknown man. Finally in the early-morning hours he'd chucked the line he'd been feeding himself about feeling responsible for her because he had been the one to awaken her passion. Responsibility had nothing to do with the feelings churning inside him, he admitted. He'd been flat-out jealous because he wanted Kim for himself. A fact he intended to make clear to Kim the first chance he got.

Only, he never got the chance until late that afternoon—thanks to a bout of flu that had swept through the office and left the clerical staff at half-force. His own pressing workload hadn't helped. Finally, near the end of the workday he got his chance, when Kim came in with a folder of documents requiring his signature.

As he began signing the documents, he was sharply aware of her nearness, her scent. "I tried to reach you this weekend," he told her.

"I know. I got your messages when I got home last night. By then it was too late to return your call."

"Did you and your friend have a nice weekend at the beach?" he asked, not bothering to hide his irritation.

Kim wrinkled her brow. "How did you know I'd gone to the beach?"

"Your neighbor Lucy told me."

"You spoke to Lucy?" Kim asked, her surprise evident.

"Yeah. When you didn't answer the phone, I thought you might be avoiding me. So I went over to your place. Imagine my surprise at learning that you and your boyfriend had gone away to the beach for the weekend."

"My boyfriend?"

"Dammit, Kim. Don't play innocent. Lucy told me he was the same guy who came by for you a couple of weeks ago. What I don't understand is if you were already involved with somebody, then why in the hell did you make love with me?"

Kim opened her mouth, closed it, and Justin watched in fascination as those blue-green eyes of hers turned stormy. She walked away from him, then turned back. "First off, I don't owe you any explanations, Justin Connelly."

"I know that, but—"

"Secondly, I was not and have not been involved with anyone except you."

He narrowed his eyes. "What about the guy with the tight buns?"

"The tight...Lucy," she said.

"That's right," Justin told her. "He made quite an impression on Lucy."

"*Every* man makes an impression on Lucy," Kim countered. "And in this case, the man happened to be the driver for the limo service your sister Tara uses. Evidently she requests a particular driver whenever she engages the service—such as the night of the auction and again this weekend when she invited me to join her at the beach."

"You were with my sister?"

"That's right. I called Tara to thank her again for inviting me to the fund-raiser. When she mentioned that she had some things she needed to handle for Alexandra's wedding and was searching for a sitter, I volunteered. So she insisted that I join them at the beach for the weekend. Since I didn't have any plans, I accepted."

Feeling like an idiot, Justin sank down in his chair. "Kim, I'm sorry. I thought—"

"I know exactly what you thought. Now if you'll excuse me, I have a ton of work to do."

Work proved to be a panacea. Because of the bout of flu that had hit the office, Kim stayed too busy the rest of the week to brood over the mess she'd made of her personal life and her relationship with Justin. She could only be grateful that business had kept Justin away from the office a great deal of the time and she'd managed to avoid any further encounters with him. What she could no longer avoid was the fact that she was seriously late for her menstrual cycle.

Opening the pregnancy-test kit she'd purchased the previous evening, she followed the directions. A short time later she held her breath as she checked the test strip for the results.

Pink.

She was pregnant.

Kim sank to the chair at her kitchen table as myriad emotions rushed through her. Excitement. Fear. Happiness. She was going to be a mother. She thought of Tara's little boy, recalled how good it had felt to hold him in her arms. Imagined how it would feel to hold her and Justin's child.

Justin.

She sobered as she thought of him. How was she going to tell him? What would he say? Maybe she didn't have to tell him. She and the baby could go away, start a new life somewhere else. Just as quickly she dismissed that notion. Justin deserved to know he was going to be a father, and their child deserved to know about him. She'd grown up without a father. No way could she put her own child in that situation.

Her head spinning, Kim took a deep breath. First things first, she decided. She needed to make an appointment with her gynecologist and have the pregnancy confirmed. Then she would decide how to tell Justin. A quick glance at the clock told her she'd have to hustle to make it to the office on time. She'd call and make an appointment the first chance she got.

The first chance she got didn't come until late that afternoon. "Doesn't Dr. Stevens have anything available tomorrow?"

"I'm sorry, Miss Lindgren, but Dr. Stevens doesn't have any openings until next week. If it's an emergency—"

"No. No, it's not an emergency. But would you take my name in case there's a cancellation? I'd really like to see her as soon as possible."

"Of course."

When she hung up the phone, Kim wondered how she was going to be able to wait until next week to find out if she was really pregnant. And how did one go about telling one of Chicago's wealthiest and most eligible bachelors that he was going to be a father? At the buzz of her intercom, Kim tried to quell her rising sense of panic and concentrate on getting through the rest of the day.

"I'll need you to make me five copies of the contracts and the exhibits for my meeting," Justin told her a short time later.

"I'll take care of it," Kim said, and started to leave.

"Kim, are you all right? You seem...distracted. If it's because of the things I said earlier this week, I've already apologized. And if you'd just let me—"

"Justin, I really don't want to get into this now," she told him.

He came around the desk, touched her shoulder. "I've been trying my best not to push you. But dammit, sooner or later we're going to have to deal with what's happening between us. It isn't going to go away."

"I know," she admitted. "But not now. Please."

"All right," he said, and released her.

Kim hurried out of his office, fearful she'd start blubbering and tell him everything if he kept being so nice to her. How could she accept his kindness when she was on the verge of turning his entire life upside down?

She made her way to the copy room on automatic pilot, scarcely aware that the office was nearly empty now. To her relief, so was the copy room. Grateful not to be forced to make small talk with anyone, she went about feeding the documents into the machine. Lost in thought, it took Kim a moment to register that the click she'd heard was the door to the copy room closing. She whipped around and spied

Robert Marsh standing in front of the closed door, a smirk on his face. "If you're waiting for the copier, I'll be finished in a minute," she said.

"Take your time," he said and moved toward her. "You know, Kim, you really ought to ditch those prissy little suits. After seeing your assets displayed so nicely at the charity auction, it seems a shame to hide them."

"When I want your fashion advice, I'll ask for it," Kim told him, and turned away. Eager to leave, she began gathering her documents from the sorter bins.

"I could give you a lot more than fashion advice," he said, his voice suddenly closer. "For instance, I bet I can satisfy a hot little number like you better than Justin Connelly can."

Kim flinched when she felt his hand brush her hair. Hugging the copies against her like a shield, she whirled around and said, "You put your hands on me again and I swear I'll break your fingers. Now get out of my way."

"What's the matter? My name's not Connelly so I'm not good enough for you? Well, I'm about to marry a Connelly, so that should be worth something."

"Get out of my way," Kim ordered again, not liking the angry glint in Marsh's eyes.

"Not until I sample some of what you've been giving to Connelly."

Suddenly realizing how vulnerable she was, Kim started to shove past him. Robert blocked her path. And when she took a step back, she came up against the worktable. The grin on Marsh's lips as he moved in turned Kim's stomach. "Back off," she ordered.

He grabbed at her. The papers she held scattered like confetti as Kim tried to pry his hands away from her face even as she aimed her knee where it hurt a man most. Robert dodged her attempt to cripple him with a well-directed knee. Laughing, he said, "You're feisty. I like that in a woman."

Angry and more than a little frightened, Kim groped the table behind her for a weapon and closed her fingers around the staple gun. When he came at her again, she wielded the weapon like a sword. "Back off, Marsh. Or I swear I'll use this on your head."

"You know, I think you just might," Robert told her, and swift as lightning he clamped his hand around her wrist and sent the stapler crashing to the floor.

Kim nearly whimpered at the pain in her wrist, but fear-induced adrenaline had her go at his face with her free hand. She raked her nails down the side of his face, had the satisfaction of him crying out.

"Why you little bi—"

And then Marsh was being yanked backward, his body slammed against the wall by Justin, who proceeded to smash his fist against Marsh's jaw.

Marsh swung out, grazed Justin near his eye. Justin barely flinched. Within moments Marsh's body grew limp. Justin whipped his gaze to Kim. "Did he hurt you?"

"No," Kim told him. "I'm all right. Let him go."

Finally Justin released him, and a moaning Marsh slumped to the floor. "Do you want to press attempted-rape charges?" he asked her.

"No."

"Consider yourself lucky, Marsh. Now get out of here before I change my mind and give you the beating you deserve," Justin told him.

Robert scrambled to his feet and swiped at his bloody nose. "I didn't try to rape her. She came on to me. She tried—"

Justin grabbed him by his shirtfront, got in his face and

said, "Shut up, Marsh. Shut up before I rip that lying tongue right out of your head and feed it to you."

"But, Justin—"

"I said to get out!" Walking over to the worktable, Justin grabbed the phone and punched the number for security. "This is Justin Connelly. Send someone up here to the copy room to escort Robert Marsh from the building."

"You can't do that," Robert objected when Justin hung up the phone.

"That's where you're wrong, pal. You see, I can do just about anything I damn well please."

Two security officers arrived at the door. "Mr. Marsh, if you'll come with us, please."

Marsh jerked his arms free. "You won't get away with this."

"Watch me. What do you think Alexandra is going to say when I tell her what happened in here tonight?"

Despite the blood oozing from his mouth, there was no mistaking the cockiness in Marsh's smile. "And just who do you think Alexandra is going to believe? The little gold digger who's sleeping with her boss? Or the word of the man she loves and is about to marry?"

Kim caught Justin's arm when he started for Marsh again. "Please, Justin, let him go. He's not worth it."

"Get him out of here," Justin told the officers.

And once they were alone, he closed his arms around Kim and held her.

Nine

"Justin?" Kim murmured against his chest.

"Give me a minute." He continued to hold her close, quelling the violence that had gripped him upon seeing Marsh manhandle her. When he finally had some measure of control over the emotions running rampant through him, he eased his hold on Kim. With a gentleness that belied the fury that he was struggling to hold in check, he cupped her face in his hands. "Are you really okay?"

"Yes," she whispered. "Your hand," she said, pulling them away from her face and looking horrified at his bruised knuckles.

"Forget about my hand," he said, and caught her fingers. "I want to know how long Marsh has been after you."

Kim lowered her gaze. "This is the first time he's ever tried anything physical," she admitted. "Until now, he's been content to spread rumors."

"Rumors?"

"About you and me. How I was out to trap you."

He tipped her chin up so that he could see her eyes. "Why didn't you tell me? I would have handled him. I could have put a stop to it. And you can bet that I'll have a talk with the staff and—"

"No. That would only make matters worse. Please swear you won't say anything."

"All right," he conceded. "But I don't like it. It's not fair to you."

"Maybe not, but ignoring the rumors is the best way to let them die down."

She was probably right, Justin reasoned. But it did nothing to alleviate his own guilt. "I'm sorry. For what Marsh did to you. For putting you in this position in the first place."

"It's not your fault. I made the decision to go on the sailing date with you, and I knew by going that I'd be leaving myself open to speculation."

"You went as a favor to me," he argued.

"I went because I wanted to go. I don't have any regrets, Justin. But maybe…maybe it would be better for everyone if I resigned."

"No," Justin said firmly.

"But what about Robert Marsh? And your sister?"

"I'll handle Marsh. And if my sister Alexandra has any sense, she'll dump the guy when I tell her what he's done."

"But—"

"I don't want you to go. I need you," he told her, panic swiftly replacing some of his earlier fury. "What would I do without you?"

"Justin, you'll have no problem getting another assistant and—"

"I want *you*."

Tears filled Kim's eyes, and she turned away, but not before the first tear slid down her cheek. In all the time he'd worked with Kim, he'd never seen her cry. That he had caused her to cry now made him feel lower than the belly of a snake. "Please, don't cry. Sweetheart, whatever's wrong, I'll fix it," he promised as he turned her to face him.

She shook her head and the tears continued to fall. "Not even you can fix this."

"What is it?" he pleaded, hating to see her in such distress. When she still said nothing, he pressed. "Tell me. I promise there's nothing you can say that will shock me."

"I think I'm pregnant."

She'd shocked him, Justin admitted, and it took him a moment before he could regain command of his tongue. By then he had processed the information. "You said you 'think'. Does that mean you aren't sure?"

She nodded. "I did one of those over-the-counter pregnancy tests and it came back positive. I have an appointment with my doctor next week just to be sure. But I've never been this late before."

"We'll get married."

The words simply popped out, shocking him as much as they obviously had shocked Kim, given her expression.

"You can't be serious."

But he was serious, Justin realized. Suddenly it all made perfect sense to him. He had never been so tied up in knots over a woman the way he had been with Kim. He cared for her—more than he could recall ever caring for another woman. "Why not?" he responded. "It makes perfect sense. We like each other, enjoy each other's company. And we've already proven that we're sexually compatible. The fact that you're carrying my child is just one more reason why we should get married."

"I don't know," she hedged, a sadness in her voice that affected him far more deeply than her tears. "Marriage is a big step."

"So is having a child," he argued. "I don't want to be a part-time father, Kim. I want to be part of my child's life. And after what you told me about your own childhood, growing up without a father, I would think you'd want the same thing for our baby."

"I do," she said.

Even though Justin knew he hadn't been completely fair to use that particular argument, he'd done so because he realized that he honestly did want Kim as his wife. He tipped her chin up and said, "Marry me, Kim."

"I…" She looked away. "Why don't we wait until I see the doctor?"

"But—"

"Please, Justin. We need to wait."

"All right. But as soon as you see the doctor, we start making plans. I'd like us to get married as soon as possible."

Kim didn't respond to that. Instead she stepped back and made a show of looking at the scattered papers on the floor of the copy room. "Look at this mess. I'd better start clearing this up."

"Leave it," Justin ordered.

"But you'll need these for your meeting in the morning."

"I said leave it." Catching her arm, he urged Kim to her feet. "I'm going to take you home."

"That's not necessary."

"It's necessary for me," he informed her, guiding her out of the copy room. After retrieving her purse, he led her to the elevator.

"But what about my car?"

"I'll have it delivered. No more arguments, Miss Lindgren," he said, and silenced her with a quick kiss. "I'm taking you home."

* * *

Justin took her home and insisted on seeing her inside. And once he'd made it through the door of her apartment, he set about taking care of her. He fixed her tea, called and ordered Chinese takeout from a nearby restaurant. While they waited for the food to arrive, Kim suggested, "Let me look at your hand."

"It's fine."

But he allowed her to bathe his bruised fist. "Thank you for coming to my rescue tonight," she said as she swabbed ointment on the scrapes. "No one's ever fought for me before."

"If it hadn't been for me, you wouldn't have been in the situation to begin with. I ignored my instincts about Marsh. I let his relationship with Alexandra cause me to turn a blind eye to what my gut told me about the man."

She applied a bandage over the worst of the damage to his hand. "All done," she said. Glancing up, she found his eyes trained on her. He looked so intense, so fierce, Kim's pulse fluttered. "Does your eye hurt very much?" she asked as she put away the first-aid kit.

"Only when I breathe," he said, making her laugh.

The doorbell sounded, and Kim latched on to the distraction. "That, I believe, is dinner."

"You sit down," Justin told her. "I'll handle this."

He handled everything.

After lighting the candles on her coffee table, he spread out a feast of tempting dishes on the glass-topped table and escorted her to one of the cushions he'd removed from the couch. Sitting beside her, Justin insisted on teaching her to use the chopsticks.

Thirty minutes later she was still laughing at her own inability to master the two wooden sticks sufficiently. "I'll never get the hang of this," she confessed.

"Then I guess I'll just have to feed you," he told her.

Which he did. All the while Kim had the feeling she was

being seduced. There was something erotic and sexual about the way he'd feed her a bite, then take a taste himself. Even as her hunger for food became sated, new hungers sprang to life inside her. Not trusting herself, Kim held up her hand when Justin lifted the chopsticks to her lips with another bite of mandarin chicken. "No more. I'm stuffed," she told him. And her senses were on overload, too, she admitted.

"All right." He put down the chopsticks. "But you still need to have a fortune cookie." He chose one, handed it to her. "Go ahead. Open it."

Kim hesitated. As much as she hated to admit it, she was superstitious, and as a rule she shied away from things like fortune cookies, tarot cards and palm readings. "Why don't I save it for later?"

"You can eat the cookie later, but don't you want to at least read your fortune? Maybe you're going to find out there's this tall, auburn-haired fellow in your future," he teased.

Kim laughed. "You don't really believe these things, do you?"

He smiled and crossed his heart. "Absolutely. Now quit stalling and read it."

Kim broke the cookie in two and removed the slip of paper.

"Come on, read it to me," he said when she simply stared at the fortune.

She swallowed, then read the inscription, "'Great happiness awaits you.'"

"Sounds good to me," Justin said.

"What does yours say?" Kim asked, afraid to give much credence to the fortune but unable to stop herself from doing so.

"Let's see," Justin said, and removed the slip of paper from his cookie. "It says, 'A wise man turns chance into good fortune.' Makes sense to me.'' The teasing glint in his eyes died and was replaced by something darker, more intense. ''It doesn't take a wise man to know that your becoming pregnant and marrying me is going to prove to be my good fortune.''

''It's getting late,'' Kim said. She stood and began clearing away the remains of their dinner.

Justin sighed. ''I guess that's my cue to leave,'' he said, and helped her carry the paper cartons to the kitchen.

Once everything was cleared away, Kim walked him to the door. ''Thank you again for everything.''

''I'll see you in the morning,'' Justin told her, and before she could respond, he took her face in his hands and kissed her. ''Dream of me.''

Kim dreamed of him. That night, and the next. And when she wasn't dreaming of Justin, she was thinking of him.

If anyone questioned Robert Marsh's abrupt departure on out-of-town business so close to his wedding date, she didn't hear about it. Justin had claimed it was for his sister's sake that he'd kept quiet about what had happened that night. He didn't want Alexandra to hear of her fiancé's actions before she'd returned to town and Justin spoke with her personally. But Kim suspected that was only half-true. She suspected he'd also wanted to protect her.

In fact, he'd even used not trusting Marsh to come after her again as an excuse to spend time with her during the next several days. That's why it took her a while to realize that Justin had insinuated himself into her life as completely as he had. He took her to a ball game at Wrigley Field, determined to teach her the art of baseball. He showed up on a rainy evening with an armful of old movies and the makings for fresh popcorn. He cajoled her into flying a kite with him, and she'd dragged him through several museums. He'd wheedled her weakness for chocolate brownies out of her and had surprised her with some from her favorite bakery one morning. She'd discovered firsthand what a difference he'd made after meeting the boys he worked with at the youth center. She'd learned he was enthralled with anything sports-related and a sucker when it came to stray kittens. And the more time she spent with him, the more deeply she fell in love with him.

One day spun into another and yet another still. Being an only child, she had grown up accustomed to being alone, to not sharing her days and nights with someone. Justin had changed that. In the space of little less than a week, he had woven himself into her life until she'd come to expect him there. While he took care not to cross the line at the office, she'd catch him looking at her across a room in such a way that made her body go hot, made her want to forget what her head said and to listen to her heart.

When he kissed her good-night, Kim's body came alive, yearned for his touch. That he didn't attempt to make love to her again when it was obvious that he wanted her confused her as much as it reassured her. The only thing that had kept her from dragging him to bed herself was that Justin had never once said that he'd loved her. Sure he'd asked her to marry him, and he made no secret of the fact that he wanted her. She believed him when he said he respected her. And she didn't doubt his sincerity when he talked about the life they could have together, with their baby. But never once did he offer her what she wanted most—his love.

Kim stared at her desk calendar, noted she only had two more days before her doctor's appointment. Once she knew the pregnancy test had been accurate, she would need to give Justin an answer to his marriage proposal.

Maybe she could love him enough for both of them, she reasoned. He desired her. She didn't doubt that. Could desire turn into love?

The phone buzzed on her desk, jarring Kim from her deep thoughts. "Kim Lindgren," she answered.

"What are you still doing there?"

"Justin," she said, unable to keep the smile from her voice. "You've only had three calls since the last time you phoned me. Mr.—"

"I'm not calling for my messages. I'm calling to tell you to close up shop and get over to my place. Or did you forget I'm fixing you dinner tonight?"

"I didn't forget," she told him.

"Then shake a leg. I'm already missing you."

Justin hung up the phone and smiled to himself as he realized he'd told Kim the truth. Although he'd only been away overnight, the need to see her was like a fever in his blood. He didn't question it. He simply accepted it. Just as he simply accepted that he would be able to convince Kim to marry him.

He never doubted that for a moment, Justin told himself as he lit the candles on the table and turned on the music he'd selected. Once he'd dealt with that scumbag Marsh and waded through the roller coaster of emotions he'd experienced at finding out Kim was pregnant, he'd been able to logically approach the problem of convincing Kim to marry him. She loved him. In hindsight he had realized that fact. Kim was not the sort of woman who slept with a man unless her heart was involved. The way he saw it, her loving him was a point in his favor. The fact that she was pregnant with his child was another. And she wanted him as much as he wanted her.

Not making love to her this past week when he'd wanted to so desperately had been one of the most difficult things he'd ever had to do, Justin admitted. But when he made love to her again, he wanted it understood that they would soon be man and wife. Justin stood back, surveyed the scene. Satisfied, he patted his pants pocket for the ring box. Now all he needed was Kim.

At the sound of the doorbell, he smiled.

Justin was still smiling when they finished dinner, and he led Kim out onto the terrace. "Would you like a sweater?" he asked.

"No, I'm fine." She stood at the railing and looked up at the sky. "It's so beautiful."

"Yes, it is," he said as he joined her.

She slanted a glance at him. "I was talking about the sky."

"I was talking about you."

Kim flushed, then turned to look up at the sky again. "I don't think I've ever seen so many stars at one time before. And the moon. It's what my mother used to call a lover's moon."

The CD player clicked to another tune, this time something even softer, more romantic. Justin touched Kim's arm. "Dance with me."

She went into his arms. Justin didn't even question how right she felt there, how perfectly her steps matched his as he danced her around the terrace beneath the moonlight. When the song ended, it seemed the most natural thing in the world to kiss her. And when he lifted his mouth, looked down at her lovely face, he said, "Make love with me."

"Yes," she whispered.

Justin didn't hesitate. He scooped her up into his arms and carried her into his bedroom, where he lowered her to the bed. And slowly he began to undress her. Unlike the night at the lake cottage, there was no storm darkening their surroundings. He wasn't forced to view her through the shadowed light of candles. Tonight moonlight spilled through the opened window to mingle with the soft glow of the lamp from the bedside table, bathing Kim in an ethereal glow.

Because he knew the thrill that awaited him when he joined his body to Kim's, the desire to take her greedily and lose himself in her was even sharper than it had been that first time. Which made him all the more determined to go slowly now, to awaken Kim to the pleasure he could bring her, to brand her with the feverish need as she had branded him that first night.

So he took his time. He released the catch at the back of the dress she'd worn. Turning her around, he unzipped the floral silk inch by inch, kissing his way down her spine as he bared her flesh. When the dress fell in a puddle at her feet, he slid his arms around her and pulled her against him so that her rear was nestled against his hardness.

"Justin," she whispered, her voice thready, her breathing labored.

Keeping her back to him, he kissed her neck and slid his palms up from her midriff to just below her breasts. He opened the clasp at the front of her bra and, brushing the lace aside, he closed his palms over her breasts. Kim's whimper spiked his need and sent blood throbbing through his veins.

Justin plucked at the nipple of one breast while he smoothed his other palm down her belly. Her muscles quivered beneath his hand as he slid his hand beneath her panties and cupped her. He eased a finger inside to test her, and when he found her warm and moist and ready for him, his control began to fray.

"Justin, I..."

"Don't fight it. Take it," he commanded as he held her against him and stroked her, brought her to the peak, urged her to go over.

Sweat beaded across his brow as he took her up again, listened to her cries of pleasure, felt her convulse around his fingers. She reached behind her, fumbled with his zipper until she freed him. When she closed her fist around him, Justin groaned. Before he could catch his breath, she began to coax him. The feeling of her soft fingers rubbing his hot flesh against the silk of her panties was maddening. And when he didn't think he could wait another moment longer, he stripped away the silk barrier that separated them. Making a place between her legs for himself, he entered her from the rear.

He stilled at her gasp, fearful that he had shocked her. Then she shocked him by beginning to move slowly, encouraging him. Using his finger, he found that sensitive spot at her center again even as he continued to move in and out of her from the rear. He felt her body strain as he increased the tempo, and when she stiffened, then shuddered in release, the last thread of his control snapped and he followed her over the cliff.

Later, when he could think again, Justin looked over at Kim lying beside him in the bed and realized he had never felt this content before. It was as though being with her had filled some emptiness inside him that he'd been unaware had been there. She made him complete somehow. He thought about the baby and imagined the three of them building a life together.

And he realized he hadn't given her the engagement ring.

"Is something wrong?" Kim asked, obviously sensing the change in him.

"I was just thinking this isn't exactly how I planned for things to go this evening."

"No? I had the distinct impression when I arrived tonight and saw the candlelight and heard the soft music that this is exactly what you had planned."

Justin grinned. "Let me rephrase that. I wanted to make

love with you, hoped that we would make love. But I had something else I'd wanted to do first."

"Something else?"

He laughed at the look in her eyes and gave her a swift kiss on the lips. "Not that. I bought you something today and I wanted to give it to you before we reached this stage in the evening."

The laughter disappeared from her eyes. "You don't need to buy me gifts."

"It's not exactly a gift. More like a promise." He groped the floor beside the bed for his pants and wrestled the box from the pocket. He held out the black velvet box to her. "Aren't you going to open it?"

Kim opened the box. "Oh, Justin."

"If you don't like it or would rather a gold band instead of the platinum, we can change it."

"No. It's beautiful. It's the most beautiful ring in the world."

He removed the emerald-cut diamond from the bed of velvet. He took her left hand in his and looking into her eyes, he slid the ring onto her finger and said, "Marry me, Kim."

"I..." Tears welled up in her eyes. "Justin, I can't take this. At least not yet. We agreed we would wait until I saw the doctor and confirmed the pregnancy."

"That's just a formality. We already know that you're pregnant with my child, and I'm asking you to be my wife," he argued.

"We still need to wait," she insisted. "I'm seeing the doctor the day after tomorrow. If he confirms I'm pregnant, then I'll marry you."

When she started to remove the ring, Justin caught her fingers and closed them. "Keep the ring. Because you are going to marry me."

Ten

She was dreaming.

Kim knew it was a dream, but smiled anyway as she imagined Justin's lips brush lightly across hers, felt his hand caress her hair. Keeping her eyes closed tightly, she stayed in bed and tried to hold on to the dream a few moments longer.

"I wish I could stay here with you, but I've got to go."

Kim snapped open her eyes and stared up into Justin's face. "You're real," she told him, touching his cheek.

He smiled and kissed her fingertips. "Sure am."

"I thought I was dreaming."

"Hmm. Was it a good one?" he asked, peeling the sheet away and exposing her bare breasts.

"Yes," she gasped as he took her in his mouth.

Lifting his head, Justin sighed, then he covered her. "Damn, I wish I could stay. But I've got over a two-hour drive ahead of me. If I don't leave now, I'll be late for my meeting.''

Kim glanced at the clock and, holding the sheet around her, sat up. As she did so, she felt a slight ache in her stomach and made a face.

"What's wrong?" Justin asked, concern darkening his hazel eyes.

"Just a little indigestion, I think. Must have been your cooking," she teased.

"You weren't complaining last night," he reminded her.

"I was being polite."

"A likely story. But since you're casting aspersions on my cooking talents, you can cook dinner tonight."

"All right," Kim conceded. "It's a date. But right now you need to go, and I need to get moving or I'll be late for work. I have a real slavedriver for a boss."

"Slavedriver, huh? Just for that, Miss Lindgren, be prepared to work a lot of overtime tonight when I get back." He kissed her again, then took her hand and stared at the ring he'd insisted on putting on her finger last night. "It looks good there."

"Yes, it does." It did look good on her finger, Kim thought, her heart swelling with love for him. When she glanced up and saw the glint in his eyes, she laughed. "Go."

"All right. I'm going. I'll call you later," he promised, and then he was gone.

Alone in Justin's apartment, Kim hugged the pillow to herself, breathed in his scent. She envisioned herself waking to Justin like this every day, sharing his bed, his home, his life.

She pressed her hand to her still-flat stomach, thought of the life growing inside her. Would he want more children with her? she wondered. She hoped so. She'd hated being an only child. And she could already imagine a little boy and girl with his auburn hair and her blue-green eyes. Smiling, she pulled back the covers, and the light reflected off the diamond in her ring. Kim stared at the ring on her hand, recalled the way Justin had looked at her when he'd put it on her finger and asked her to marry him.

The only thing that had been missing was him saying that he loved her. For a moment she felt an ache in her chest that he hadn't given her the words. Just as quickly she cut off the negative thoughts, refusing to allow anything to intrude on her happiness. Tossing aside the covers, she headed for the shower.

While she showered, she thought of Justin. So maybe he didn't love her the way she loved him, but he did care for her. She was sure of that. And they did have a baby to consider. Their child. It would be enough. It *was* enough, she amended. She would be a good wife to him, be a good mother to their child, Kim promised herself as she shut off the shower and slipped on Justin's robe and went in search of her clothes.

She found them scattered on the floor of Justin's bedroom. When she found herself reliving how her clothes had ended up on the floor, Kim laughed aloud at herself. Justin wasn't the only one in danger of running late this morning, she thought as she dressed and hurried out the door. Unless she planned to show up at Connelly Corporation wearing last night's dress, she needed to hustle to get to her apartment and change clothes before going to work. Feeling another twinge, Kim pressed her fingers to her middle. Evidently Justin's tomato sauce really hadn't agreed with her, she thought, and made a mental note to remember to grab a few antacid tablets from the medicine cabinet.

Kim headed for the medicine cabinet the moment she got home. She reached for the bottle of antacid tablets and, after reading the label to be sure it was safe to take during pregnancy, she popped a few into her mouth. While she chewed the chalky tablets, she quickly changed into a lightweight persimmon dress. Reaching for her hairpins, she started to put her hair up in its customary twist, then opted to leave it down instead.

Reluctantly she removed the ring from her finger and tucked it inside her purse. Even though the gossip had died down at the office, she knew there was no way the diamond on her finger would go unnoticed. Besides, she intended to accept Justin's proposal, but she had promised herself and him that she wouldn't do so until the pregnancy was official. Once it was, she would need to brace herself for the reactions at the office, she realized. Strangely, the thought of doing so didn't bother her nearly as much now as it had a short time ago. Grabbing her purse and keys, she headed off to work and prayed that by the time she arrived at Connelly headquarters those antacid tablets she'd taken would have begun to do their magic.

But they hadn't. Nor did the tablets she took when she arrived at the office. After an hour into her day, the slight twinges she'd experienced that morning had become a bellyache. Becoming alarmed, Kim made a trip to the ladies room. Her blood ran cold when she discovered she had begun to spot.

No, Kim told herself, as she fought back the panic that threatened to paralyze her. She'd read that pregnant women sometimes experienced some spotting. It didn't mean she was having a miscarriage. But fearful that she might be, she hurried back to her office and, after shutting the door, called the doctor.

"This is Kimberly Lindgren," she said. "I have an appointment to see Dr. Stevens tomorrow afternoon, but I need to see her today. Right away."

"Is this an emergency, Miss Lindgren?"

"Yes. Yes, it is. I'm…I'm pregnant. Or at least, I think I am, and I've begun to spot."

After answering several questions, she hung up the phone. As calmly as she could, she notified the receptionist that she was leaving and started for the doctor's office.

By the time she'd arrived at the medical complex, the spotting had become a warm flow of blood. Sobbing, she sat across the desk from Dr. Stevens following her exam. "You're sure it wasn't a miscarriage?" she asked the woman who had been her gynecologist for the past five years.

"I'm positive, Kim. There was no baby."

"But the pregnancy test I took…"

"They aren't always accurate. While they're right most of the time, occasionally they give a false positive reading. I'm afraid that's what happened in your case."

"But I was so late. And I've never been that late before," Kim explained. While she was glad there had been no miscarriage, she felt as though she had just lost her baby all the same.

"I can't give you a reason why this happened now, Kim. You said you've been under a great deal of stress, perhaps your cycle being late is your body's way of reacting to that stress." Dr. Stevens handed her another tissue.

"Thank you," Kim murmured, trying to get a handle on her emotions.

"From your reaction, I assume that had you been pregnant you would have wanted the child."

"Yes," Kim told her, knowing that the doctor was referring to her unmarried status. "I would have wanted it." Only now did she realize just how much she had wanted the baby, how much she had begun to think of it growing inside her.

"I'm sorry, then."

Kim nodded, wiped at her eyes.

"The good news is that you're a healthy young woman. There's no reason you can't conceive a child in the future."

"Yes, I'm sure you're right," Kim said, and stood. "Thank you for seeing me so quickly, doctor."

"Not a problem. Those samples I gave you should help with the cramping. If it doesn't, let me know and I'll phone in a prescription for you."

"Yes. Thank you again," Kim said. But she didn't think there was anything the good doctor could give her to ease the ache in her heart. As far as she knew, no one had yet discovered any magic pill to wipe away the pain of losing one's dreams.

Kim managed to find her car in the parking lot. Once she was inside, she rested her head against the steering wheel and began to cry.

She was still crying when she drove past Connelly Corporation headquarters and when she arrived at her apartment. She spied the flashing light on her answering machine and ignored it. She didn't want to speak to anyone. Not yet. Not when her pain was still so sharp.

Unable the bear the cheery sunshine spilling through the windows, Kim went from room to room and yanked closed all the drapes in the apartment. Then she retreated to her bedroom, where she turned off the telephone ringer and left her dress on the floor where it fell. She crawled beneath the covers, curled up into a ball and began to sob. She sobbed deeply, her chest shaking with the depth of her grief.

She grieved because there was no baby growing inside her, because there would never be Justin's baby growing inside her. She grieved for what the two of them might have shared and never would. And she grieved because there would be no Justin in her life. Not even from a distance as he had been before, because she couldn't possibly remain at Connelly Corporation now. As she thought of all the dreams that would never come true now, she continued to cry until there were no more tears left. And when the tears finally stopped, she slept.

When Kim awoke, the apartment was in total darkness and there was a pounding inside her head. Sitting up, she felt almost drunk, and it took a few minutes to orient herself. A glance at the bedside clock told her it was past eleven o'clock at night. She'd obviously crashed, Kim reasoned. No wonder since she'd gotten little sleep the previous night at Justin's place.

Justin.

Suddenly the memories came slamming back. Justin giving her the engagement ring, asking her to marry him. Then today, her finding out there was no baby, that she hadn't been pregnant at all. Pain sliced through her like a jagged blade, making her ache all over again.

The pounding started again, and she held her head. Finally she realized the pounding was at her door. Scrambling from the bed, she began flipping on lights and made her way to the front door.

"Kim!" Justin shouted, as he beat against her door.

"You sure you don't want me to call the police? That's what they do on the detective shows," Lucy Brown informed him.

"Lucy, I—"

Kim opened the door. "Justin? What on earth—"

Justin caught her by the shoulders and nearly lifted her off her feet. "Are you all right?"

Taken aback by the wild look in his eyes, it took her a moment to find her voice. "Yes," she finally managed, stunned to see him looking such a wreck. His tie was askew, stubble darkened his cheeks and his hair looked as if it had been styled with a pitchfork.

Before she could ask him what was wrong, he muttered, "Thank God." Then he pulled her into his arms and kissed her. The desperation in his kiss surprised her, because she couldn't imagine anything that would cause him such distress.

"I don't suppose there's any point in calling the police now," Lucy said.

Justin ended the kiss, but his eyes never left Kim's. "No, no point," Justin told the older woman. "Thanks, anyway. I think I've got things under control now."

"Looks like it to me," Lucy commented, then disappeared into her own apartment.

"Are you all right? Were you in some kind of an accident? Did something happen at the office? Is that why you left early?"

He fired the questions at her, and Kim wasn't quite sure where to start to answer. So she said, "I'm all right. And nothing happened at the office. Not the way you mean. I just needed...I needed to come home."

"But I called you here. I left at least half a dozen messages and then the machine stopped picking up. If you were here, why didn't you answer the phone?"

"You'd better come inside, Justin. We need to talk."

The knot that had formed in Justin's stomach when he'd called the office and learned that Kim had left early took on the proportions of a boulder. Now that the worst of his fears—that she'd been injured or in some terrible accident—had been dismissed, he could see that something else was wrong. Seriously wrong. Even without the benefit of growing up under the same roof with three sisters, he'd been in the world long enough to know that when a woman said "We need to talk," whatever it was she was going to tell him, he wasn't going to like.

He followed Kim inside, spied her purse and keys lying on the floor beside her shoes. She was always so neat and orderly, it seemed out of character for her. Just as her leaving the office early without any explanation had been totally out of character for Kim. Justin noted the droop in her shoulders as she walked over to the table and switched on the lamp. And that feeling that something terrible had occurred increased tenfold.

"I know it's late," she said, turning around to face him. "But would you like a drink? Or maybe some coffee?"

Justin strode over to her, tipped her face to the light and swore. Dark smudges lay like bruises beneath her eyes, and her cheeks were streaked from what he suspected were dried tears. "I don't want a drink or any coffee. I want to know what's wrong. What's happened?"

"I went to see my doctor today," she told him in a voice that seemed devoid of life.

His heart, already in a vise, suddenly felt as though someone had reached inside him and squeezed it even tighter. "Are you all right?" he asked, and led her to the couch to sit down, but continued to hold her hand. "Sweetheart, why didn't you tell me you were sick?"

"I'm not sick," she informed him, and tugged her fingers free.

He dropped his gaze to her stomach, noted the way she was hugging her arms around her middle. "The baby?" he asked, his heart in his throat. "Is something wrong with the baby?"

"There is no baby."

Justin felt as though he'd been coldcocked. A dozen different emotions hit him at once, savaged him. "Did you..."

He swallowed, worked through the red haze of fury and tried again. ''Did you terminate it?''

Kim's head jerked up, and for the first time since he'd walked into the apartment, there was a spark of life in her eyes. ''There was no baby. I was never pregnant.''

''But the pregnancy test—''

''Was wrong,'' she said. ''One of those one-in-a-zillion or whatever the figure is that's wrong. I'm not pregnant. I never was.''

Stunned, Justin was barely aware of Kim standing and walking over to retrieve her purse from the floor. He continued to sit there on her couch as he tried to digest what she'd told him.

There was no baby. There never was a baby.

So why did he feel this sudden sense of loss?

Because he had begun to think of himself as a father, he realized. He had begun to think of himself as a husband— of him and Kim and their baby as a family.

''I was going to call you tomorrow and give you the good news. And return this.''

Justin looked up to where Kim now stood before him, holding out the engagement ring he had put on her finger the previous night. He rose, looked into her eyes. ''Is it good news, Kim?''

''Sure,'' she said. ''You offering to marry me when I thought I was pregnant...it was very noble of you, Justin. A lot of men in your position wouldn't have been willing to take responsibility and sacrifice their freedom. It meant a great deal to me that you were willing to. But now,'' she said, her voice catching, ''it's not necessary. So I'm returning the ring.''

It was that catch in her voice and the shimmer of fresh tears in Kim's eyes that gave Justin hope. He stood, but made no attempt to take the ring she held out to him. "I thought you liked the ring."

"I did. I do," she amended.

"Then why are you giving it back?"

She squinched her brows together the way she did when she was trying to work out a puzzling problem. "Didn't you hear me? There's no reason for us to get married now."

"Sure there is. When two people love each other, when they want to spend the rest of their lives together, getting married is generally what they do. At least that's what my parents did. And I figure if it's good enough for them, it's good enough for us."

"You love me?"

"Yes," Justin told her, realizing it was true. "And unless I'm mistaken, you love me, too. Don't you?"

Kim nodded.

Taking the ring from her, he took her hand. "So will you marry me, Kim Lindgren? Will you be my family? Make babies with me? Grow old and gray with me?"

"Yes," she told him.

He slid the ring onto her finger, kissed it. "I love you, Kim."

"And I love you," she said, and offered her mouth to him.

Justin kissed her deeply with all the love in his heart. And when he lifted her into his arms and asked her where the bedroom was, she showed him.

Much later as he lay in bed with the woman he loved in his arms, Justin's stomach grumbled. "That reminds me. You still owe me dinner."

Laughing, Kim raised herself up on one elbow. "I seem to recall offering to fix you a snack a few hours ago, and you insisted all you needed was to hold me, that you didn't need food.''

''What can I say? My heart says one thing, but my stomach says another. Right now the stomach is winning the battle, and it's none too happy that I skipped dinner.''

''You never did say what happened that caused you to be so late.''

Justin frowned. ''Alexandra came back to town this evening, and I went by to see her.''

''You told her about Robert.''

''Yes,'' Justin said, his jaw tightening as he thought of the other man.

''She must have been devastated.''

''She was upset. I mean, she has to feel like a fool, seeing how Marsh has been using her.''

''I can't even begin to imagine how she must feel,'' Kim told him. ''She must be terribly hurt.''

''I guess. But I'm not sure if it was her heart that hurt so much as it was her pride.''

''Did she say what she's going to do?''

''I know what she should do,'' Justin informed her. ''She should dump him and be grateful she found out what a low-life he is before she married him.''

''But I take it that's not what Alexandra plans to do.''

Justin sighed. ''She said she wanted to talk to Marsh first before she makes any decision.''

''Well, you'll know soon enough. The wedding is only three days away.''

''Two,'' Justin corrected, and pointed to the window where the sun was beginning its rise. He looked at Kim, thought of the new life they were beginning. ''I'd like you to come with me this morning and tell my parents our news. And as much as I want to shout out to the world that you're going to be my wife, we probably should wait until we see what Alexandra is going to do first.''

''Justin, how do you think your parents are going to feel about this? About us?''

''Sweetheart, they're going to love you as much as I do.''

Justin had been right, Kim realized as Emma and Grant gave her a hug the next evening upon their arrival at the family's Lake Shore home. His parents had seemed thrilled over their engagement when they'd told them the news the previous day. But not wanting to steal any of the limelight from their daughter, they had agreed with Kim and Justin to keep the news quiet until after Alexandra's wedding.

''I can't believe she's still going to marry the guy,'' Justin told Kim as he brought her a glass of wine. ''You'd think that after I told her what he tried to do to you she'd have given him the boot. Instead she's going to marry him tomorrow. There's got to be something I can do to make her see it's a mistake.''

''You've done everything you can. It's your sister's decision, Justin. Not yours.''

''Yeah. Well, I'm tempted to have the guy shanghaied and shipped to Daniel in Altaria so she can't marry him.''

Kim placed a hand on his arm. ''Your brother Daniel has enough worries.''

''You're right,'' Justin said, and squeezed her fingertips. ''Have I told you lately that I love you?''

''Not in the last five minutes.''

Emma came over to them. ''I can hardly wait to tell Lilly and Tobias your good news,'' she told them.

''I hope they'll be pleased,'' Kim said, somewhat nervous at the prospect of telling Justin's grandparents about their engagement.

"They'll be thrilled. Just as Grant and I are thrilled," Emma assured her.

"Emma, what on earth is keeping Alexandra?" Lilly demanded as she made her way over to them.

"I'll send Ruby to check on her," Emma offered, and escaped to dispatch the housekeeper to see what was keeping Alexandra.

"Grandmother, let me help you to your chair," Justin offered.

"Quit fussing over me," Lilly told her grandson. "Just because I have to use this cane doesn't mean I'm addlepated. Why don't you go get me a sherry while I talk to your young lady?"

Lilly turned her deep-blue eyes on Kim. "So, Kimberly, are you in love with my grandson?"

Taken aback by the woman's candor, Kim hesitated a moment. But there was no mistaking the sharp mind behind those eyes. "Yes, I am."

She nodded, apparently satisfied with the answer. "How do you feel about babies?"

Kim nearly choked on her wine. "I like them."

"Good," Lilly said, and smiled.

"Miss Emma." Ruby came rushing down the stairs and headed for Justin's mother.

"Now, I wonder what has her all aflutter," Lilly said.

"Ruby, for heaven's sake. What is it? What's wrong?" Emma's voice held concern.

"It's Miss Alexandra. She's gone."

"Gone?" Emma repeated.

Ruby held out a sheet of paper. "She left a note. She says she's sorry, but there isn't going to be any wedding, and that she's going away for a while."

"My poor baby," Emma said as she took the note from Ruby, read it and passed it on to her husband.

"Hey, what's going on?" Tara asked as she entered the room. "What's all the fuss about?"

"It's Alexandra," Kim explained. "She's gone. She left a note saying that the wedding is off."

"It's my fault," Justin told his family, and relayed his conversation with Alexandra the previous evening.

"I always knew that guy was a louse," Tara said. "Alexandra's better off without him."

"I agree," Justin told them. "I'll admit I wanted her to dump Marsh, but I never meant to hurt her."

"I'm sure your sister knows that," Emma assured her son.

"The truth is, I thought she took it pretty well," Justin advised his family. "I mean, I thought it was more a question of her pride being hurt than her feelings. She didn't act all broken up when I told her what Marsh was up to."

"Of course the girl wasn't broken up," Lilly interjected. "Any fool with eyes in his head could see that the girl wasn't in love with that scoundrel Marsh."

"I think your grandmother's right," Emma replied.

"Of course, I'm right. All a body had to do was see them together to know that they weren't in love with each other," Lilly informed them.

"Tell me, Grandmother," Tara began, a sly look in her eyes. "Just exactly how do two people look when they're in love with each other?"

"The way you and that Paige boy used to look at each other. The same way your brother and his young lady look at each other now." She shifted her gaze to Justin and Kim. "All you have to do is see the way that boy looks at her to know he's in love with her."

"You're right, Grandmother," Justin said laughing. "I am in love with her."

"And I love him," Kim replied, seeing no point in denying it since she'd already told the lady.

"So what do you intend to do about it?" Lilly asked her grandson.

"I'm going to marry her," Justin informed his grandmother.

"Soon, I hope. Your grandfather and I are getting tired of waiting for more great-grandchildren."

"As soon as I can," Justin replied.

"And those great-grandchildren?" Lilly prompted.

"We intend to get to work on them right away."

*   *   *   *   *

DYNASTIES: THE CONNELLYS continues....
Turn the page for a bonus look at what's in
store for you in the next Connellys book
—only from Silhouette Desire:
THE ROYAL & THE RUNAWAY BRIDE
by Kathryn Jensen
July 2002

One

It wasn't that he disliked royal functions. Phillip Kinrowan had grown up in aristocratic circles, attended his first ball before he'd been able to walk, ridden his first Grand Prix champion jumper at Monaco before he turned six and owned an estate by the time he'd cleared the hurdles of puberty. He simply hated advertising the fact he had a title because of the attention it got him. Attention that often resulted in trouble. Female trouble.

He was reminded of those dangers as he stepped forward to be announced by the page before the crowd of beautiful people. "The Kingdom of Altaria welcomes His Highness, Phillip Kinrowan, Prince of Silverdorn!" The page's voice rang out in Italian, French and English, in deference to the American-born king in whose honor the celebration was being held.

As he descended the grand curving staircase, Phillip was already bored. Except for the Americans, the same faces greeted him at nearly every function. Perhaps among Daniel Connelly's family Phillip might find someone of interest to talk to. His glance drifted down the receiving line, finding no one to spark his curiosity until the end.

A young woman, her raven hair trimmed almost boyishly short, stood awkwardly behind the guests of honor. She wore an elegant gown that matched the vivid green of her eyes. The way her eyes shifted restlessly around the vast, chandeliered room, not even bothering to hide her impatience with the pomp and circumstance, told him she was a kindred spirit.

Just who was she? As he watched, she nudged the woman in front of her, whispered something in her ear, then hiked up her billowy skirts in both fists and hightailed it for the doors leading to the garden. In a flash she was gone, but he was chuckling to himself at the parting image of chunky brown boots, laces dangling loose, revealed beneath layers of satin and chiffon. A little rebel—how charming!

As if drawn to her, Phillip followed the young woman off the stone balcony to a formal garden, baking in Mediterranean heat even after the July sun had set. He caught a glimpse of emerald fabric whipping around a corner of hedgerow that separated the stables from the manicured greenery.

"Hey, you there, wait up!" he called, breaking into a run.

But if she heard, his shout had no effect. When he emerged from the shrubs to stand at the edge of the exercise yard, there was no sign of the woman.

A low whinny and snort caught Phillip's attention, and he whipped around, moving toward the sound like a cat stalking its prey. Ducking into the dark interior of the stable, he spotted her on the lowest rail of a stall, reaching over to stroke the nose of a pure white horse.

"Does the stable master know you're messing about with one of his most valued mounts?" he asked.

She jumped and snapped her hand back but recovered quickly, tipping her nose into the air. Her green eyes flashed defiantly at him. "Of course. He asked me to look in on him."

"He did, did he?" He grinned, even more curious about her now. From a distance, she'd been intriguing. Up close she was dazzling. "And why would he do that?"

"Because I'm...I'm a trainer. He asked me to work with—" her gaze shifted almost imperceptibly to the bronze plaque on the stall's half door "—with King's Passion."

"A trainer," he repeated, thinking that might well account for her mixed attire and uneasiness in a formal setting. "You're an American."

"Yes," she said, hopping backward off the rail. "I work for the Connellys but came as a favor to lend a hand at the royal stable for the celebration."

"I see," he said. "So you've had a lot of experience with horses."

"Oodles." She flashed him a cocky grin.

He walked around her, checking out her body without hiding his intent. He guessed she'd look damn fine straddling one of his jumpers, and the image excited him.

"I have a problem horse in my own stable. Maybe you could break free of your duties here and take a look at him."

"I would, of course, but I'm terribly busy here. And I won't be staying all that long."

"Too bad. I would have paid you well." No reaction. "And treated you to a fine lunch. My cook makes a bouillabaisse to die for."

Now her pretty eyes widened. He'd found a weakness. Food.

"Tell you what," he said quickly. "I'll speak to our soon-to-be-crowned king before the end of the evening. Perhaps he can spare you for a few hours tomorrow or the next day. You give my jumper a quick inspection, and I'll treat you to the finest seafood in the Mediterranean."

"All I can spare is an hour or two at most." She was studying him for the first time, and he felt as if she suddenly had him under a magnifying glass.

"Are you always so serious about accepting work?" He was delighted to see her eyes soften when they at last met his. For once he allowed genuine warmth to enter his own expression. After all, she was safe, not some husband-hunting debutante or social climber.

The corners of her lips lifted tentatively. "Not always." She crossed one booted foot over the other, still considering him. "Make it tomorrow afternoon. You don't have to ask Daniel Connelly for permission. I'm free to make my own decisions."

"Good, I'll send a car for you around one o'clock. First work, then luncheon."

Alexandra kicked herself all the way back to the ball-room. What had possessed her to accept Phillip Kinrowan's invitation to his estate? Sheer hunkiness, that was it! He was the handsomest man she'd ever laid eyes on. And, on top of his looks, he owned a stable full of horses.

From the time she'd been a little girl, she'd adored the creatures. Unfortunately, they didn't always return her affection. Unless you could count as tokens of endearment all those bruises and fractures she'd suffered during lessons when she was a schoolgirl.

So, what had possessed her to tell Kinrowan that she was

a trainer? A childhood fantasy, perhaps? Still, she should be all right. She knew enough about horses to fake her way through an hour or two of horse-related conversation.

Alexandra shook her head, lifting her skirts and clomping in her boots up to the patio. Well, it would be a kick, anyway. And spending a few hours around a man who obviously had no interest in her other than professionally, and probably had tons more money than her father, couldn't possibly hold the usual threat men had been to her. What the hell...maybe an afternoon with Phillip Kinrowan would help her forget. Help her start to wash away the terrible pain, and stop thinking about the reason she'd run away from Chicago, from her friends, and the bitterest disappointment of a young woman's life.

DYNASTIES: THE CONNELLYS

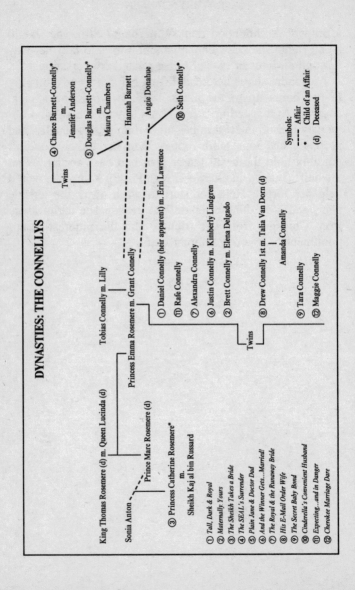

King Thomas Rosemere (d) m. Queen Lucinda (d)

Sonia Anton

Prince Marc Rosemere (d)

Princess Emma Rosemere m. Grant Connelly

Tobias Connelly m. Lilly

④ Chance Barnett-Connelly*
m.
Jennifer Anderson

⑤ Douglas Barnett-Connelly*
m.
Maura Chambers

Twins

Hannah Barnett

Angie Donahue

⑩ Seth Connelly*

③ Princess Catherine Rosemere*
m.
Sheikh Kaj al bin Russard

① Daniel Connelly (heir apparent) m. Erin Lawrence

⑪ Rafe Connelly

⑦ Alexandra Connelly

⑥ Justin Connelly m. Kimberly Lindgren

② Brett Connelly m. Elena Delgado

⑧ Drew Connelly 1st m. Talia Van Dorn (d)

Amanda Connelly

⑨ Tara Connelly

⑫ Maggie Connelly

Twins

① *Tall, Dark & Royal*
② *Maternally Yours*
③ *The Sheikh Takes a Bride*
④ *The SEAL's Surrender*
⑤ *Plain Jane & Doctor Dad*
⑥ *And the Winner Gets...Married!*
⑦ *The Royal & the Runaway Bride*
⑧ *His E-Mail Order Wife*
⑨ *The Secret Baby Bond*
⑩ *Cinderella's Convenient Husband*
⑪ *Expecting...and in Danger*
⑫ *Cherokee Marriage Dare*

Symbols:
- - - - - Affair
* Child of an Affair
(d) Deceased

And now turn the page
for a sneak preview of
BEHIND THE MASK
the exciting new novel by
Metsy Hingle
On sale in December 2002
from MIRA books.

One

"I'll pay you one million dollars to find my wife."

"All right," Michael Sullivan replied from the other end of the phone line. "You've got my attention."

Adam Webster smiled in satisfaction at the ex-cop's change in attitude. "I'm glad to hear that," he said as he gazed at the view of the Miami skyline afforded him from his penthouse suite. He was glad, but he wasn't at all surprised. He'd learned a long time ago that money talked—even to a man like Sullivan. A man who, according to his sources, had been among Houston's best and brightest police detectives five years ago when he'd resigned abruptly following his partner's death. Now he hired himself out as a detective, bodyguard or bounty hunter—whatever the situation called for. The man was said to be as mean as a rattlesnake and twice as dangerous. He also reportedly had the instincts of a bloodhound when it came to tracking down someone who didn't want to be found. It was Sullivan's latter skill that he needed now to find Lily. "You've been a difficult man to get in touch with, Mr. Sullivan," Adam said, making no attempt to hide his displeasure. "My assistant tells me she's left you several messages. Did you receive them?"

"Yeah, I got the messages, but I've been out of town finishing up a case. The truth is the only reason you caught me in my office is because I had to swing by to pick up some reports I needed for the case I'm working on now."

"I see," Adam said tightly. "I'm not accustomed to being ignored, Mr. Sullivan."

"No one's ignoring you, Webster. But since I'm pressed for time, why don't we dispense with my lack of manners and you tell me why you're willing to pay me a million dollars to find your wife."

"Because she's missing," Adam said sharply, angered by the man's insolence. Biting back his temper, he reminded himself that he needed Sullivan to find Lily. With temper making him edgy, he turned away from the sweep of windows and stalked over to his desk. Sitting down, he picked up the framed photo of Lily. Frustration rushed through him that he had yet to find her. "I understand your expertise is finding people, Sullivan. I'd like to hire you to find my wife."

"How long has she been missing?" Sullivan asked.

"Six months." And after six months it still gnawed at him like a festering sore that he had underestimated Lily as he had. He detested mistakes, refused to tolerate them. Yet he had made a mistake by underestimating Lily.

Never in a million years would he have believed that sweet, docile Lily—the girl he'd fed, clothed and molded into a woman worthy to be his wife—would have the guts to defy him. To steal his gun. To shoot him. Even more infuriating was the fact that she'd not only gotten away from the idiots he'd hired to guard her, but that he'd doled out a considerable sum of money to private detectives and some not so reputable business associates to find her. And though they'd come close to grabbing her twice, she had still managed to get away. But not for much longer, Adam promised himself. If Sullivan was half as good as the reports on him indicated, Lily's rebellion was about to come to an end.

"Webster? You still there?"

"Yes. Yes," Adam repeated, dragging his thoughts back to the present. "What did you say?"

"I asked if you've filed a missing persons report with the police?"

"No," Adam advised him. "I didn't want the police involved. I still don't."

"Why not?"

"Aside from the fact that I can do without the publicity, I don't want any charges filed against my wife."

"Last I heard, it wasn't a crime for a woman to leave her husband," Sullivan informed him.

"No. But shooting me, kidnapping my son and stealing cash and jewelry from my safe *are* crimes. If I had brought the police into it, they would have issued an arrest warrant for Lily. I'd prefer to handle things myself."

Sullivan swore.

"My sentiments exactly," Adam told him.

"Why didn't you say up front that she stole the kid?" the other man demanded, but before Adam could answer, Sullivan asked, "How old's your boy?"

Adam frowned a moment while he calculated how old the kid would be now. "Two."

"Damn! That's got to be rough, him being so little and you missing all that time with him."

"It is," Adam said because it was obvious that Sullivan expected it. But in truth, he didn't give a damn about the little brat. He never had. As far as he was concerned his problems with Lily began with the kid. Not insisting that she terminate the pregnancy had been a major screw-up on his part—one he would make sure didn't happen again. But first…first he had to get Lily back. "I'd like you to start looking for them right away, Mr. Sullivan. If you'll come by my office, say within the hour, I'll provide you with any information you'll need and give you a retainer for your services.''

"I'm afraid I can't make it today."

"Why not?" he demanded, unaccustomed to having his requests denied.

"Because at the moment, I'm handling a matter for another client."

"And is this other client offering to pay you a million dollars for your services?" he demanded.

"No."

"Then I suggest you tell him or her to find someone else to handle whatever it is you're doing."

"That's not the way I work," Sullivan said, his voice dropping to a chilling growl. "When I make a commitment to do a job, I do it. I've got to go. I'll give you a call when I get back, and if you're still interested in hiring me, we'll talk."

When the dial tone buzzed in his ear, Adam slammed down the telephone receiver. "Arrogant bastard," he muttered, clenching his hands into fists. Sullivan would pay for that, he promised. As soon as the man found Lily for him, he would make him regret his insolence. Shoving away from the desk, he headed to the bar and poured himself a shot of bourbon. He tossed it back, felt its sting as it slid down his throat to his gut like liquid fire. After pouring himself another one, he grabbed the crystal tumbler and stalked across the ultra-modern office that he'd spent a small fortune decorating. Ignoring the polish finish on the black marble desktop, he set down his glass and picked up the silver-framed picture of Lily again. He stared at her— the pale, delicate skin, the silky blonde hair—and felt the violent punch of lust. Reaching for the bourbon he tossed back another swallow, all the while staring at Lily's face.

Lily belonged to him. She had from the moment he'd first set eyes on her. Even at fifteen and still an innocent, she'd left him breathless and aching. She'd been worth ten of her mother. It was the reason he'd saved her. Were it not for him, she'd have probably hooked up with some two-bit punk and been selling herself on the streets of Miami before she'd turned sixteen.

Instead, he'd rescued her from her wretched life. He'd provided for her education, showered her with gifts, and when she'd been legally an adult he had married her. He hadn't had to make Lily his wife to bed her, Adam reasoned. Any number of women would have killed to be in her position, just for the chance to be in his bed. He knew he looked good, Adam admitted. He took care of himself, kept his body in shape and could easily pass for twenty years younger. Hadn't he heard a woman in one of his clubs call him a stud just last week? He could have had his pick of women to marry, but he'd chosen Lily. His breath turned to a pant as he thought of taking Lily that first time, of thrusting himself into her warm, tender flesh. And the memory made the throbbing in his groin even more painful.

He slapped down the glass and reached for the phone. "Kit, it's Adam," he said when the line was answered at the Miami nightclub. "How's that new girl working out, the young blond with the southern drawl you introduced me to last week?"

"You must mean Annabelle," Kit said, her voice cool and sultry. "She's working out fine. A little shy, but the customers seem to like her. She's a fast learner and very eager to please. She should be here in a few minutes."

"Send her up to the penthouse when she gets there," he said, already anticipating the feel of the pretty, young girl beneath him. "And Kit, get someone else to take her shift tonight. She's going to be busy."

After hanging up the phone, he reached for his glass and started to go to the bedroom adjoining his office to wait for Annabelle. But his gaze fell on Lily's photo again. He lifted his glass in a mock salute. "It won't be long now, Lily," he whispered before downing the remainder of the bourbon. He would use Sullivan to find her, and once he had her back, he'd see to it that Lily never dared to defy him again.

As for Sullivan, the man was in need of a lesson in respect—which he personally intended to see that he got.

Silhouette *Desire*

presents

DYNASTIES:
THE
CONNELLYS

A brand-new miniseries about the Connellys of Chicago,
a wealthy, powerful American family tied by blood to the
royal family of the island kingdom of Altaria.
They're wealthy, powerful and rocked by
scandal, betrayal…and passion!

Look for a whole year of glamorous and
utterly romantic tales in 2002:

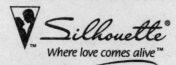

Silhouette

Where love comes alive™

Visit Silhouette at www.eHarlequin.com

SDDYN02

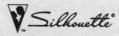

Continues the captivating series from
bestselling author
BARBARA McCAULEY

SECRETS!

Hidden legacies, hidden loves—revel in the
unfolding of the Blackhawk siblings' deepest, most
desirable SECRETS!

Don't miss the next irresistible books in the series...

TAMING BLACKHAWK
On Sale May 2002
(SD #1437)

IN BLACKHAWK'S BED
On Sale July 2002
(SD #1447)

And look for another title on sale in 2003!

Available at your favorite retail outlet.

Where love comes alive™